To
Christina DuBois
*

Cheryl Osolinski
*

Cortney Osolinski
*

Veterans and First Responders
*

To all who do not allow their lives to be defined by disabilities

CONTENTS

PROLOGUE

A Lifetime of Adventures is a novel. The characters are completely fictitious. Any references to individuals and businesses are fabricated to provide a foundation for sustaining the story line.

The idea that an individual with distinct disabilities chooses to live life to the fullest and refuses to be defined by any specific disability can be a reality for some. *A Lifetime of Adventures* highlights the belief and tenacity of the author's grandniece who is, in fact, blind yet reasons there is nothing she cannot do. She is currently a teacher with an earned graduate degree. She enjoys snow skiing, with a certified ski instructor as a guide.

My grandniece, Cortney Osolinski, provided the following comments upon reading A *Lifetime of Adventures*:

> Uncle Jimmy, we really enjoyed reading your upcoming book! We loved traveling through the good times, hardships, blessings, and joys with Timothy Sands. So much excitement with the kidnapping, the war, and the aftermath... We were surprised when several tragedies happened that those involved were not more devastated, but learning of their strong faith in God made it easy to become an Overcomer. Tim was surrounded with people who lifted him up, gave him confidence, and didn't do everything for him but helped him figure out how to do it for himself.
>
> I recognize this when reading the book because it's familiar in my life. Since I was born blind and with multiple disabilities, I, too, am

an Overcomer! I have been blessed with wonderful family, friends, and mentors throughout my life. "With God, all things are possible!" And with the right philosophy and attitude, anyone can become an Overcomer. I don't think of myself as disabled; I think I'm unique. And I wouldn't change a thing.

Growing up, I felt lucky to be blind. When I was little, I would sneak my braille book under my covers, lay it on my belly, and read with my fingers. Mom would take a peek in the dark room and think I was sleeping. I grew up riding a three-wheel bike and now a bicycle built for two. I snow ski, hike, kayak, rock climb, travel, start the family campfires, and I can cook the best ramen noodles you've ever had! If I wasn't blind, I may not have had the opportunity to achieve a master's degree and become a teacher of the blind and visually impaired. And there's nothing more rewarding than helping others to be happy and successful. I do need to ask for assistance for certain things, but I find I can do most things everyone else can do, just in a different way.

Thank you for sharing your manuscript with us. We feel honored. Mom and I are both very inspired by this book!

PS: remember, they didn't have power bars in the late '50s. I think it should be an apple. Ha-ha!

Part 1

The Adventures of a Young Person

It's a dangerous business, Frodo, going out your door.
You step onto the road, and if you don't keep your feet,
there's no knowing where you might be swept off to.

—J. R. R. Tolkien

CHAPTER 1

Timothy was the youngest child of Robert and Margaret Sands. Brother John and sister Sandra called him Timmy, but he preferred to be simply called Tim. His father, Robert, would call his youngest son Tim, but Mother would only call him Timothy. When Tim was ten years old, the Sands family was heading to Muncie Valley, Pennsylvania, for a week of vacation. The Sands were joining up with five families to share in an annual group vacation at Cooper's Camp.

Pastor C. W. Cooper owned a mountaintop home along with several outbuildings. The location earned the title "Cooper's Camp" because several families would vacation together in a truly camping atmosphere. Usually, the adults would occupy the camp house, and the children would sleep in the various cabins. The cabins for the boys were small, with only two bunk beds each. The cabins for the girls were larger with four bunk beds each. The camp had one large building which was affectionately called the mess hall. The mess hall was semienclosed and featured picnic tables and a couple of homemade wood- or charcoal-fired grills. The refrigeration system was simply large metal tubs filled with blocks of ice and topped with wooden lids.

The camp had one deep water well. The well had an eight-inch iron casing. The only method of obtaining water was to lower a torpedo-shaped canister down the well. The canister had a leather flapper attached on the bottom of the canister. When the canister was lowered, the flapper would allow the water to enter the canister. When the canister was raised by a rope on a pulley, the flapper would close, and most of the water would make it to the surface. The water would then be transferred from the canister into buckets.

The families who vacationed together worked together. The shopping, cooking, cleanup, and water gathering were duties shared by all. The meals in the mess hall were nothing less than amazing. The cooks would begin the day with iron skillets, filled with bacon. Lunch was simply sandwiches. Dinner would be a variety of grilled burgers, steak, fish, or hotdogs. Some of the cooks were creative and somehow baked bread, cakes, and brownies. Sometimes, the smell of the cooking overpowered the actual taste of the meals.

Cooper's Camp provided a vacation experience that included opportunities for hiking, fishing, swimming, or just rocking on the porch while enjoying the mountain scenery. The kids would play board games and ball games or go scavenge hunting for arrowheads. The one and only camp experience, which was not enjoyable, was the necessary use of an outhouse.

The Sands family vacationed at Cooper's Camp every summer. John, Sandra, and Tim knew the camp rules. No one leaves the cabin after dark. No one leaves the outhouse without a sufficient amount of paper rolls. You couldn't call it toilet paper, because there was no toilet. Everyone knew the rule that no one runs away from a bear. What John, Sandra, and Tim did not know was what would be their reading assignments for this vacation. Without failure, Margaret Sands would set the reading rules for their family vacations. Everyone was expected to read at least one book of the Bible and one book chosen by Mother.

As the Sands family was approaching the mountains, Margaret opened a book bag she had positioned on the floor of the car by her feet. "Okay, guys, here's what I have for you this year. Our theme for this year is adventures. I have some classic adventure books. Everyone is expected to read the book of Acts. This reading will give us all a better appreciation of missionaries establishing churches. On our trip home, I will ask questions of these missionary adventures. John, I also have for you the *Call of the Wild*, by Jack London. Sandra, you have the *Swiss Family Robinson*, by Johann David Wyss. Timothy, you have the *Adventures of Huckleberry Finn*, by Mark Twain. Dad has the *Last of the Mohicans,* by James Fennimore Cooper. I have the *Hobbit*, by J. R. R. Tolkien. I also have something new this year. I have a journal for each of us. I want everyone to begin establishing a journal."

Tim asked, "Mom, how do I establish a journal?"

Margaret handed Timothy a leather-bound book. Tim was excited to find the brown soft-leather-bound book had his name embossed on the front lower-right corner of the book cover.

"Wow!" said Tim. "My own book with my name." When he found the pages in the book completely blank, he said, "Mom, the pages don't have any words."

Margaret said, "Timothy, a journal is a book that you write in every day."

"What do I write?"

"You can write anything you want. You can record events, things you did or didn't do, thoughts, or impressions."

Tim said, "What if nothing happened that day?"

Margaret said, "Timothy, just give it a try. You will find that something usually happens. In time, you will find the journal to be something precious."

Tim was captivated with his new book, which had his name embossed in gold letters. About fifteen minutes later, Tim said,

"Mom, thank you for my book. I can't wait until tomorrow. I hope I can find something to write in my journal."

About ten minutes passed and Tim said, "Mom, I have something to write in my journal."

Margaret said, "Timothy, you don't need to tell us what you write in your journal. It can be private."

Tim said, "Mom, I want to write something about you and Sandra."

Sandra said, "Dad, tell Timmy to keep me out of his journal."

Tim said, "Mom said I can write whatever I want."

Margaret asked, "Timothy, what could you possibly want to write about Sandra and me already?"

Tim said, "When Dad drives up the road to Cooper's Camp, you and Sandra will freak out when he drives around the hairpin turn and the narrow road with the cliff side. You both will scream and demand that Dad stop and let you out of the car so you can walk. I want to record this as part of our adventure."

Sandra said, "Dad, tell Timmy to keep me out of his journal."

Robert said, "Okay, everyone, quiet."

CHAPTER 2

COOPER'S CAMP MAIN HALL

Cooper's Camp was at one time a hunter's camp. Some men from Cooper's church still travel up to the camp for hunting. In addition, some of the men would travel up early during the hunting season to do some construction, repairs, or general upkeep of the buildings.

John said, "Dad, do you think I could come up with some of the men during hunting season this year?"

Robert said, "I don't have a problem with that. What do you think, Margaret?"

Margaret said, "The only problem I have is, why are these trips only open to the men?"

Sandra said, "Count me out. I don't like the outhouse in the summer. When it gets cold, I don't want to even think about using a cold wooden seat."

Robert said, "I think a group of us ought to plan a work week and do some major repairs to the mess hall. Maybe even upgrade the kitchen to include a real stove and some refrigeration units."

The Sands were arriving at the approach road to Cooper's Camp. Robert had to stop at a designated area where all arriving cars needed to stop and make sure no one was coming down the approach road. The road had to be clear of any traffic because the road was only a single lane. It was impossible for two cars to pass each other on the road. If two cars came upon each other, the car travelling up the mountain road would need to back down. It would be impossible for the descending car to back up the mountain. When Robert was comfortable that no cars were descending, he proclaimed, "Okay, let's go."

The 1954 Mercury hummed as Robert dropped into a low gear and steadily climbed the mountain road. Sandra closed her eyes. Margaret's hands turned white as she gripped the armrest with one hand and covered her mouth with the other. John and Tim were half hanging out the windows while looking down the cliff and laughing at how close the car was to the edge.

Sandra cried, "Dad, tell them to shut up."

Suddenly, Robert came to an abrupt stop and said, "Oh, great." Standing in the middle of the road was a huge black steer. Apparently, the steer had broken loose from its farm on the opposite side of the mountain. A farmer maintained two or three fenced-in plateaus on the mountain. Fortunately, the steer decided to walk up the road and seemed to be returning to its farm. Unfortunately, Robert had lost all momentum with the car. He now needed to gun the engine, and the drive wheels began spinning and kicking up gravel and stones, which generated screams from Margaret and Sandra.

The remainder of the trip up the mountain was uneventful. However, Margaret and Sandra were quick to get out of the car when Robert pulled into the parking area. They both made a beeline to the famous outhouse, which had a double seat.

The Sands family was the first of the five families to arrive. This fact gave Robert and Margaret the advantage to pick out and claim the best bedroom in the house. Sandra picked out her favorite lower bunk bed in the girl's cabin. John and Tim chose the top bunks in one of the newest boys' cabins.

Margaret and Robert decided to go to the mess hall to set up snacks and coffee for the arrival of their vacationing friends. To their surprise, several upgrades were already made to the mess hall. The kitchen had two refrigerators and two electric ranges. In addition, some of the picnic tables had been repaired and painted. Margaret was quick to say, "Let's make some cookies and coffee. I have everything to make some snacks. We can be the welcoming committee for our friends with fresh baked cookies."

It wasn't long before Cooper's Camp was filled with activity. The Thomsons were a family of five. The Corsons have two children, and they brought an additional friend. The Purdue family has three girls. The Owens family is the youngest family, with one small two-year-old, and looking forward to a new arrival. The Miner family is a family of four. The Lettice family is the largest family of seven. In addition, Charles Lettice is the loudest, funniest, and leader of the pack. Charles sets the pace, determines the agenda, and is loved by all. If there is any question about what to do or what to eat, Charles will make the decision. As an example, Charles organized a "head count" to establish how many people needed to be fed at meals.

Charles said, "Okay, cooks, we need to plan our meals for thirty people. That's twelve adults and seventeen kids."

Eve Thomson replied, "Charles, my dear, when I went to school, twelve and seventeen totaled twenty-nine."

Charles was quick to respond, "Eve, my dearest, please remember that Karen Owens is eating for two. The thirtieth member of our group has not yet made his or her appearance. However, we must account for his or her food consumption."

Karen Owens said, "To all my dear friends, I must make one correction with respect to my eating habits. I am not eating for two. I am, in fact, eating for three. I'm carrying *twins*."

The entire group burst in a cheer and applause. All the adults gathered around Karen for hugs.

Margaret announced, "Cookies are ready."

The kids all charged to the serving table.

CHAPTER 3

GIRL'S CABIN

The entire group of kids vacationing together was all friends. David Corson Jr. brought a new friend; he is the same age as Timothy. His name is Brett Young. David Jr. was a longtime friend with John. Therefore, David Jr. and Brett bunked in the same cabin with Tim and John.

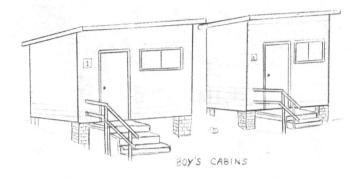

BOY'S CABINS

The boys in their respective cabins woke early. As was their custom, they ran around the girls' cabins and banged on the doors, windows, and walls to wake up the girls. The kids all gathered around the washbasins and brushed their teeth. In a matter of minutes, teams were chosen, and a game of kickball was underway.

It wasn't long before the air was filled with the smell of bacon cooking in the iron skillets. The aroma of coffee also permeated the fresh mountain air. Yes, vacation was in full play.

Charles Lettice called for the raising of the American flag. Everyone gathered around the flagpole, which was located just in front of the mess hall and on the crest of a ridge overlooking the valley. Located at the base of the flagpole was a memorial stone inscribed with the words:

> Praise to God
>
> for our
>
> freedoms and liberties.
>
> Honor and appreciation
>
> to those
>
> who defend them.

Charles raised the new American flag and then led everyone in reciting the Pledge of Allegiance.

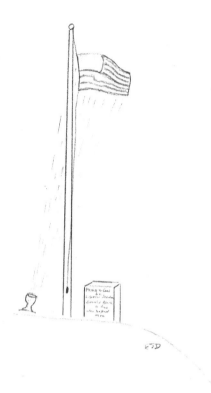

"I pledge allegiance to the flag of the United States of America and to the Republic for which it stands, one Nation under God, indivisible, with liberty and justice for all."

The American flag would remain raised and lit at night, throughout the vacation at Cooper's Camp.

Breakfast was eggs, pancakes, toast, sausage, and bacon. After breakfast, Charles Lettice announced, "Today, we go swimming down at Beaver Lake. However, we walk down by way of the farmer's road, eat hotdogs at the concession stand, and walk back in time for dinner. Bring money to buy your hotdogs, soda, and ice cream for lunch."

There was a collective and traditional response of a *hurrah* from the entire group. Charles was a marine, and over the years, he established the old "hurrah" as a means of approval for anything.

Charles had one more announcement, "Let it be known, the mother of the expected twins is excused from walking down to Beaver Lake."

Karen was quick to respond, "My dear Charles, let me remind you that you are not my father. I will make my own decisions about what I will or will not do."

The entire group let out an even louder *hurrah*.

Everyone laughed but none louder than Charles.

Robert said, "Thank you to all the cooks for a great breakfast. The cooks and team Owens, from last year, are excused from cleanup duties. All others are, hereby, designated as the cleanup crew."

The cooks and team Owens all clapped and collectively said, "Yeah."

Cleanup was relatively easy because the group only used paper plates, plastic wear, and reusable cups. Each day, everyone received a reusable cup. Each person would write his or her name on a cup and use it throughout the day. In addition, the cooks did not want anyone to touch their iron skillets, so cleanup was not a big deal. The men would all help with drawing water as needed.

Charles again made another announcement, "Let's all take the next half hour to one hour as quiet time."

The vacationers all had various expectations for their personal and family quiet time. Therefore, they had a longtime agreement that one hour a day would be set aside as quiet time.

Tim was excited about this quiet time. He ran to his cabin; grabbed his Bible, *Huckleberry Finn,* and his journal; and climbed onto the top bunk. He read from the Bible, Acts 1. He started to read from *Huckleberry Finn* and then realized that Brett was just sitting on the bottom bunk with nothing to read. He had not been prepared for quiet time.

Tim said, "Brett, did anyone tell you we had a one-hour quiet time for reading?"

Brett replied, "No. But it's okay."

Tim said, "I love to read. Look, now I have my own journal."

Brett asked, "What do you do with a journal?"

Tim said, "My mom said I can write whatever I want in the journal."

Tim then considered something and said, "Brett, do you want to read from my Bible or from Huck Finn, or both? I can share."

Brett said, "No, thanks. I am not good at reading."

Tim said, "Well, then, let's read together. Come up here."

Brett climbed up on the top bunk.

Tim smiled and said, "This is great."

Tim opened his Bible and read chapter 1 again. This time, he read it out loud. Then he read chapters 1 and 2 from *Huckleberry Finn*. Brett was focused and glued to every word. Tim was a good reader. Then Tim opened his journal and said, "Let's come up with something to write in my journal."

Brett said, "You should say we are new friends, and you read to me from the Bible and from *Huckleberry Finn*. You could say we had a great breakfast. You could say this has been the best vacation ever."

Tim said, "You said you're not a good reader, but you are a good writer. That's exactly what I'm going to write."

Page 1, August 6, 1957

Today is the first day of my summer vacation at Cooper's Camp. Yesterday, Dad drove up the mountain road, and he had to stop because a big steer was blocking the road. When Dad started again, the tires kicked up dirt and stones, and it scared Mom and Sandra. They screamed really loud. When we got to the top of the mountain, Mom and Sandra ran to the outhouse. I think the ride up the mountain scared the pee out of them.

I met a new friend. His name is Brett Young. I think we are going to be best friends for good.

Mom said I had to read the book of Acts in the Bible and *The Adventures of Huckleberry Finn*. No problem. Brett didn't bring any books, so I am reading to him.

I don't know what else to write.

Goodbye.

Overcomer

O yea, Brett said to say we had a good breakfast of pancakes and bacon. O yea, last night, Mom made chocolate chip cookies. They were really good.

Goodbye again.

Overcomer

Tim said, "My mom said what I write in my journal is private. But since you are my best friend, you can read it." Tim then handed his journal to Brett.

Brett didn't open it. He handed it back. Brett said, "You read it for me."

Tim was happy to read his first entry in the journal to Brett.

Brett said, "That's great. Can we really be best friends for good?"

Tim said, "Sure. We are already."

Brett asked, "Why did you sign off with the word *Overcomer?*"

Tim said, "My favorite Bible verse is Revelation 2:17. This verse identifies an *overcomer* as having hidden food, a white stone, and a new secret name."

Brett said, "Maybe I could be the overcomer number two."

Tim said, "No number two, three, or four. In the Bible, every-one is equal. You could be an overcomer just like me."

Brett asked, "What can we overcome?"

"Anything."

Charles Lettice brought a bullhorn to announce the end of quiet time. He then proclaimed a 10:00 a.m. departure for the swimming trip.

The entire group began their hike down the mountain around 10:00 a.m. When they reached the hairpin turn on the approach road, there was a side road used by the local farmers. This back road led directly to Beaver Lake. In about fifteen minutes on the farmer's road, the vacationers came upon a bunch of steer on the road. With all the noise made by the vacationers, the steer were anxious to make their way off the road and back into their fenced-in pasture via the holes in the fence. Apparently, the steer knew they had free access to the road anytime they wanted, but they didn't like sharing the road with this crowd of people.

As the vacationers were walking down the road, some advanced to the lead; others were walking slower. Tim was walking and holding hands with his mother.

Tim said, "Mom, Brett Young is my newest best friend."

"Timothy, that's nice. I think Brett seems like a very nice boy."

Tim said, "Mom, I really like Brett, but he doesn't like to read."

Margaret said, "Timothy, you know we have always encouraged reading. Some people just don't like to read."

"No, Mom. I think Brett can't read."

Margaret said, "Well, Timothy, you just do the best you can to be his friend."

Tim said, "That'll be easy."

The swimming trip was a great success. Everyone enjoyed the water. Charles had arranged a few group games. The best event was the egg toss. The boys teamed up against the girls. The girls won. The boys kept throwing the eggs too hard.

The return trip to Cooper's Camp was challenging. Everyone was tired from swimming and games. Now they were walking up the mountain road. Charles led the vacationers in singing some crazy songs.

The cooks prepared an Italian meal. The menu included spaghetti with meatballs, salad, bread, brownies, and homemade ice cream for dessert.

The first day of vacation ended with the kids playing board games and the adults playing card games.

Charles Lettice did not need to announce bedtime. Everyone was tired and began turning in by 10:00 p.m.

*****

Before Margaret left the mess hall, she pulled Lisa Corson aside for a little chat.

Margaret said, "Lisa, do you mind if I ask you a question about Brett Young?"

Lisa said, "Sure. I hope he hasn't been a problem."

Margaret said, "No, not at all. Timothy has proclaimed that he and Brett are now best friends for life. Timothy does think Brett has some difficulty with reading. Do you know if Brett is having problems in school?"

Lisa was quiet and seemed to wipe away a tear.

Margaret said, "Lisa, I don't wish to make you upset or uncomfortable. If you don't want to discuss this, I will totally respect your privacy."

Lisa took Margaret by the hand and said, "Yes, Brett is having problems in school. In fact, Brett is having problems in life. The problems are not with Brett. He is a good boy and is absolutely no threat to Timothy or anyone else. His family history is a mess. David and I are making plans to adopt Brett, but that is not common knowledge. We need to proceed further in the process before we can make any announcement."

Margaret said, "Is there anything Robert and I can do to help you?"

Lisa, in frustration, said, "Yeah, if you can come up with five thousand dollars. We have all the paperwork done and thought we had done everything required by the adoption agency and the state. Then wham! They hit us with an increase in finances. The bill is now five thousand dollars more than we can scrape together. Therefore, the process is on hold."

Margaret asked, "What happens if you can't pay the bill? Will you be able to take custody or care for Brett until the process is completed?"

Lisa said, "For now we can continue caring for Brett. However, at some point, the state will remove Brett and place him back into foster care. The problem is the state will not give us a firm deadline."

Margaret asked, "Do you mind if I share this situation with Robert?"

"Margaret, I was not supposed to say anything. Please don't say anything just yet."

Margaret said, "Okay, but I will not be able to help you financially unless I can share this with Robert."

Lisa said, "I understand. Really, I'm sorry I ever said anything to you because now I have burdened you with a problem and you can't do anything to help. I'm so sorry, Margaret. I never should have said anything about the money. It's just that I am so frustrated. When you asked, I just had to say something."

Margaret said, "Lisa, please know we want to help. If you can give me permission, I will talk with Robert."

Lisa gave Margaret a big hug. They walked together in silence to the main house.

Margaret had a hard time falling asleep that night. She prayed.

CHAPTER 4

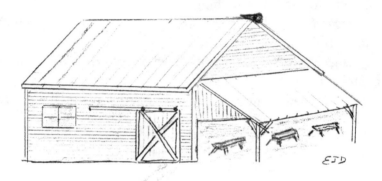

MESS HALL

Day two of vacation started off with a fantastic breakfast. Charles Lettice announced a canoe adventure down the Lazy River.

Tim was excited about reading with Brett during their quiet time. Tim read the second chapter of Acts. Tim and Brett both agreed that the chapter was a little hard to understand.

Tim said, "I will ask my mom about this chapter. She helps me understand some of the more difficult parts of the Bible. I think I understand the part about God's foreknowledge and determinate counsel. It means God knows what will happen because He has determined to make it happen."

Tim then asked, "Brett, do you want to read some Huck Finn? I can help you along the way."

Brett said, "I will try."

Tim handed Brett the book and said, "Start at chapter 2."

Brett looked at the words, and after a short time, he closed the book and handed it back to Tim. He said, "I can't. I have never read a book that was so big."

Tim said, "Okay, no problem. I will read for today."

After reading chapter 2 of *Huck Finn*, Tim said, "Brett, what do you think I should write in the journal today?"

Brett seemed to be just as excited as Tim to suggest things to write in the journal. Brett said, "Let's remember that Mr. Lettice raised the American flag. I think it's cool that people driving down in the valley can look up the mountain and see the flag. Let's remember the egg toss. I never played that game before. Let's remember how much easier it was to walk down the mountain road than it was walking back up the mountain. Let's remember that Carla won the Monopoly game last night. Let's remember we heard some dogs or coyotes howling last night. That was a little scary."

Tim said, "Brett, something doesn't make sense to me. You could write your own book, and yet you can't read. What's that all about?"

Brett said, "I can read. It's just that I get scared because I get stuck on some words and people yell at me and call me a dummy."

Tim said, "Are you saying your parents yell at you?"

Brett said, "No. I don't have any parents. Maybe someday Mr. and Mrs. Corson will be my parents. The people who made fun of me were called guardians."

Tim said, "I will not make fun of you."

Brett said, "Yeah, I know. It's just that your books are so big and I just feel overwhelmed. I could never read something that big."

Tim said, "How can the Corsons become your parents?"

Brett said, "They were trying to adopt me. That would be the greatest thing ever. But now it may not happen."

"Why not?"

"Because they don't have enough money."

Tim said, "So how much money do they need?"

Brett said, "Mr. and Mrs. Corson don't talk to me about that stuff. However, I heard them say one night they are short five thousand dollars. I don't think they will ever get that much money, on top of whatever they have already spent."

Tim said, "Brett, my mom and dad always say we should pray. Maybe we should ask God for the money."

Brett said, "I didn't know God gave out money."

Tim said, "Pastor Cooper always says we don't have because we don't ask. So let's ask. Let's pray."

Tim and Brett closed their eyes. Tim prayed, "Lord God, you know my friend Brett. We need you to give us five thousand dollars. You know Mr. and Mrs. Corson want to be Brett's new parents. They can't, unless you give us the money. Can you do this for my friend? Okay, thanks. Amen."

Tim said, "Well, that was easy."

Brett said, "Do you think God will do it?"

Tim said, "Sure. Didn't you hear *him* say okay?"

Brett looked at Tim in disbelief. Brett said, "I heard you say okay."

Tim said, "I am sure. God will do it."

Tim opened his journal and wrote,

Day 2, August 7, 1957

Our vacation at Cooper's Camp started off yesterday with the raising of the American flag. We all recited the Pledge of Allegiance. Brett suggested we remember how people driving in the valley can look up and see the flag, even at night because Mr. Lettice has a light shining on the flag.

We had a great breakfast. Everyone went swimming at Beaver Lake. Brett suggested we remember how easy it was to walk down the mountain and how hard it was to walk back up the mountain.

We played a bunch of games. The girls won the egg toss. Brett had never played that game before. The boys always seem to lose because we throw the eggs too hard.

My friend Brett and I had a talk about how Mr. and Mrs. Corson will be his new parents. We prayed and asked God to give them $5,000. I have an idea on how that can happen.

Last night, we heard some dogs or coyotes howling. It was a little scary.

Goodbye.
Overcomer

Tim read the journal entry to Brett.

Brett said, "That's a great entry. What is your idea of how God will give us the money?"

Tim said, "I will tell you later. I need to go talk to my mom."

Tim found his mother and said, "Mom, I need to do something today. Can I skip the canoe trip?"

Margaret said, "Sure. You can skip the canoe trip. However, what do you want to do?"

Tim said, "I need to go into town to the library. I want to buy a used book for Brett. I also need to make a phone call."

Margaret said, "Timothy, I trust you. I know you are trying to help Brett. What is the phone call all about?"

Tim said, "I can't talk about the phone call yet."

Margaret said, "Okay. How are you going to get to the library? I will *not* drive on that mountain road."

Tim said, "I was going to just ask if anyone is going shopping. Brett and I can hitch a ride."

Margaret said, "Okay."

Tim found Mrs. Corson and said, "Mrs. Corson, I have permission from my mom to skip the canoe trip today. Do you mind if Brett can skip the canoe trip and go with me into town?"

Lisa Corson said, "I don't care if Brett skips the canoe trip, but what is the purpose of going into town?"

Tim said, "I want to go to the library and buy a book for Brett."

Lisa Corson studied Tim for a few seconds and said, "Okay, I understand."

Tim asked around and found that Frank and Pauline Miner were going shopping. They agreed to take Tim and Brett to the Library.

Tim found Brett and said, "Brett, I set it up so that we can go into town today. We are going to the library."

Brett said, "Great. Let's go."

*****

Tim and Brett entered the library. A lady with a pleasant smile and gray hair greeted the two boys.

"Good morning, boys. My name is Linda Miller. Most people call me Ms. Linda. What can I do for you today?"

Tim said, "My name is Tim Sands, and this is my best friend. His name is Brett Young."

Tim produced fourteen dollars from his spending money. I need to buy a used book for Brett." Tim then took one dollar from the loosely folded money and continued, "I also need to make a phone call." He then handed Ms. Linda thirteen dollars in one hand and one dollar from his other hand, thus making a distinction between two anticipated transactions.

Ms. Linda studied the two boys and then said, "I think I can help you, but I need a little more information. First, what kind of used book do you want to purchase? Secondly, to whom do you want to call?"

Tim said, "Great. I knew you could help. First, my friend Brett has had some problems with his reading. He is capable of reading, and he is smart. However, he has been ridiculed and is frightened by big books. He needs a book that is fun and easy to read. Nothing too big."

Ms. Linda asked, "And the phone call?"

Tim said, "I need to call my pastor. You may need to help me find the phone number. I can give you the name of the church and town, but I don't know the phone number."

Ms. Linda said, "Please give me the name and town."

Tim said, "It's Pastor C. W. Cooper, Vineland, New Jersey."

Ms. Linda asked, "Are you vacationing at Cooper's Camp?"

Tim said, "Yes."

Ms. Linda said, "I know Pastor Cooper. In fact, I have his phone number on file. He often comes to the library when he visits his camp."

Ms. Linda went into her office and came back with a small Rolodex card. She said, "Tim, why don't I connect you with Pastor Cooper on the telephone. Then I can talk with Brett about some possible books."

Tim said, "That would be great."

Ms. Linda dialed and passed the telephone to Tim as soon as it began ringing.

Pastor Cooper answered, "Hello."

Tim said, "Pastor Cooper, this is Tim Sands."

"Well, Timothy Sands, I'm glad to hear from you. From where are you calling? I thought you were vacationing at the camp."

Tim said, "We are vacationing at your camp. We're having a great time. I am downtown at the library. Ms. Linda is allowing me to make this phone call."

Pastor Cooper said, "What is the purpose of your call? Is everything all right?"

Tim said, "I needed to call you because my best friend Brett Young needs five thousand dollars."

Pastor Cooper said, "Well, Timothy, that seems like a lot of money. Why don't you tell me about the need for this money?"

Tim said, "My friend has no family. He was living with different people. Now Mr. and Mrs. Corson are trying to adopt Brett. It seems like the Corsons can't come up with all the money. O yeah, you can't tell anybody."

Pastor Cooper said, "Tim, are they David and Lisa Corson?"

Tim said, "Yes."

Pastor Cooper said, "Now, Tim, why are you calling me? I will gladly do what I can to help the Corsons, but I certainly do not have that kind of money."

Tim said, "No, I am not asking for your money. I asked God for the money. See, Brett and I prayed about this, so God knows everything about it, and he will do it."

Pastor Cooper said, "Tim, I can appreciate your faith in God, but how do you know he will do it?"

Tim said, "He will. I also have an idea on how God can do this."

Pastor Cooper asked, "And what is your idea?"

Tim said, "Last year, you said a missionary had a need for money. You took up a wave offering. I remember how you asked everyone to look in his or her wallet and pull out the largest dollar, not the smallest. You asked everyone to wave the money and drop it into the offering plate. I remember you took an offering and raised a bunch of money. I was thinking you could do that for the Corsons."

Pastor Cooper said, "Tim, sometimes God uses different ways of providing. I'm not sure I can ask for an offering if I can't tell everyone who the offering is for."

Tim said, "The people don't need to know. God knows Brett and the Corsons. You always tell us we have not because we don't ask. Well, Brett and me asked God. I believe God is able to do it."

Pastor Cooper said, "Tim, you sure sound convinced God will provide for your friend."

Tim said, "Yes, I believe. You always said we need the faith of a mustard seed. Well, I believe bigger than a seed."

Pastor Cooper said, "Give me some time to think about this."

Tim said, "Okay, you have plenty of time because it's only Tuesday. That will give God more time to make sure everyone in church Sunday will have big dollars in their wallets."

Pastor Cooper said, "Tim, I am not yet sure your idea can be accomplished by this Sunday."

Tim said, "God can do it. We can't wait, because the state people will take Brett away if the Corsons don't pay the money."

Pastor Cooper said, "Tim, why don't you have your parents give me a call?"

Tim said, "Mom will not drive down the access road. Besides, Mom and Dad don't know anything about this. I can't tell anyone."

Pastor Cooper said, "Tim, you told me everything about this situation."

Tim said, "Yeah, because God and you are on the same team."

Pastor Cooper said, "Okay, Tim, I will see what can be done."

Tim said, "Great. Thanks."

Tim hung up the phone.

Ms. Linda had talked with Brett, and together, they selected three books.

Tim said, "Can we have all three books for thirteen dollars, or do we need to choose one of the three?"

Ms. Linda said, "I believe the fourteen dollars will cover the cost of all three books."

Tim seemed to be a little hesitant and then said, "Ms. Linda, I forgot to ask if you had a journal for Brett. My mom gave me my own journal with my name printed in gold letters on the front of the journal. I know Brett would love his own journal even without his name on it."

Ms. Linda said, "No, Tim. We would not normally keep personal journals."

Tim said, "Okay. We will take the three books."

Tim and Brett sat on a bench outside the library while waiting for Mr. and Mrs. Miner.

Brett said, "Tim, thank you for buying me these books. I have never owned a book of my own. You are my best friend."

Tim didn't say anything. He just smiled.

CHAPTER 5

Day three of vacation started with doughnuts and sticky buns. Frank and Pauline Miner had gone shopping yesterday, and they practically bought out the local bakery. Doughnuts and sticky buns with milk, juice, and coffee were the easiest breakfast.

Charles Lettice announced today's activity to be hiking and rock climbing. All those going on this adventure should gather in the mess hall at 10:00 a.m. The purpose of gathering in the mess hall was to fill backpacks with water and food to eat on the trail.

Tim and Brett climbed onto Tim's bunk for today's quiet time. Tim read Acts 3, and *Huckleberry Finn*, chapter 3.

Brett had his three new books. Brett said, "Tim, I didn't tell you how Ms. Linda helped me yesterday. She told me a story in her life on how she overcame her own problems with reading. I want to try her method."

Brett opened *The Chronicles of Narnia*, by C. S. Lewis. He took off his shoes; he then took three long deep breaths. He closed his eyes for a few seconds, and then he opened his eyes and began slowly reading out loud. Brett read all of chapter 1 with no problems at all.

Tim said, "Wow! Brett, you did a great job. What did Ms. Linda say to you?"

Brett said, "She said that sometimes we shut down from anxiety. She said this anxiety becomes worse if people criticize you. She said I just needed to relax. Take off the shoes. Breathe deeply three times. Shut my eyes for a few seconds and begin reading slowly. She said I didn't have a reading problem. She said I have an anxiety problem."

Tim said, "Maybe the anxiety will even get better after the Corsons finalize the adoption. What should we write in the journal today?"

Brett said, "I would like to remember how my best friend bought me three new books. I would like to remember how Ms. Linda gave me a key to overcoming a reading problem. That makes me an overcomer. I would like you to say what happened as a result of your phone call to Pastor Cooper, how God will help the Corsons overcome a money problem."

Day 3, August 8, 1957

Yesterday, Brett and me skipped the canoe trip. We went to the local library. I bought Brett three used reading books. I spent fourteen dollars of my spending money. Mom paid me back the fourteen dollars. Somehow, Lisa Corson found out, and she gave me fourteen dollars. I learned a lesson. Buy three books for your friend, and you can double your money! Ha ha.

The librarian, Ms. Linda, gave Brett a key to his reading problem. Actually, Brett doesn't have a reading problem at all. It looks like he has an anxiety problem. Brett took off his shoes, took three deep breaths, closed his eyes for a few seconds, and began reading slowly. Brett is a good reader.

Brett and I prayed about the Corsons' need for $5,000. God knows that Brett needs to be adopted by Mr. and Mrs. Corson. I called Pastor Cooper and asked him to conduct a wave offering at church this Sunday.

My faith is greater than a mustard seed.

Goodbye
Overcomer

Brett said, "Read it."
Tim read the journal entry.
Brett responded with a thumb up.

*****

The hiking group was primarily the kids. Only three adults were willing to climb the rocks. The total number of climbers was fifteen. Charles divided the climbers into three groups. Each group had one adult and four kids. Tim, Brett, John, and David Jr. were assigned to Mr. Richard Thomson's group. Mr. Thomson was a previous college football player and coach. Mr. Thomson was now a lawyer and a well-respected leader in our church. Team Thomson would likely take the lead in rock climbing.

The hiking adventure began with an hour walk to the base of the rock walls. During the hike, Charles Lettice tried to get the three groups to march. He did this by calling out an old military marching cadence. The so-called marching was a little sloppy but fun.

Team Thomson took the lead up the rock walls. The walls were challenging but nothing that required any serious equipment or training. The trip to the summit took about an hour. Everyone enjoyed the view from the top of the mountain as they ate sandwiches and apples for lunch.

The return trip was planned for a different path down the mountain. The walk down the mountain was much easier until they came upon a washout. Apparently, the melting snow and rains created a washout. This being August means the washout was dry. However, the washout created a gorge and presented a problem in crossing. After a few minutes of searching for the least difficult means of passage, Charles announced, "Hey guys, check this out." He then pointed to a dead tree that had fallen across the gorge at a narrow point.

Mr. Thomson said, "Crossing the gorge will be easier if we walk across the fallen tree, and if the tree is strong enough to hold one person at a time, I will take the point and see if the tree is solid enough to support us."

Mr. Thomson began a slow walk across the tree bridge. At the halfway point, Mr. Thomson jumped a little to see if the tree was strong. It held up to his test. Mr. Thomson was successful and declared it safe as he stood on the other side of the gorge. Mr. Thomson said, "Come across one at a time. Take a few deep breaths, and walk slowly. Focus on where you are stepping. Don't look around, and don't look down." The entire group of hikers successfully crossed the gorge.

Dinner in the mess hall was grilled hamburgers and chicken. Mrs. Miner made her famous German potato salad, and Mr. Miner cooked corn on the cob.

The evening was filled with board games and cards.

CHAPTER 6

Tim woke up in the middle of the night with a sharp pain in his right ankle. Tim knew he twisted his ankle while climbing the rock walls, but it didn't stop him. In fact, he didn't even limp after he twisted it. Now he could tell it was stiff, maybe swollen. Tim couldn't do anything. No one was allowed out of the cabins at night. He would just need to wait for sunup.

As soon as it became light, Tim called out for his brother. "John, are you awake?"

John responded, "I am now."

Tim said, "I need you to go get Mom."

"Why?"

"Because something is wrong with my ankle."

"What's wrong with your ankle?"

"I don't know. It hurts. It's swollen."

John didn't respond. Neither did he get out of bed.

Tim said, "John, go get Mom. Now!"

John didn't say anything, but he did get up and went out the door.

Margaret entered the boys' cabin, and Brett and David Jr. woke. Brett said, "Good morning, Mrs. Sands. What's up?"

Margaret didn't answer. She said, "Timothy, what's wrong with your ankle?"

"I guess I twisted my ankle yesterday. It didn't hurt yesterday, but overnight, it really began to hurt."

Margaret said, "Let me see it."

Tim pulled his leg out of his sleeping bag, and the ankle looked horrible.

Margaret said, "That sure doesn't look good. John, you go get Marge Thomson. She is a nurse. I want her to see this."

Brett asked, "Mrs. Sands, can I do anything?"

Margaret replied, "Yes, Brett. Please go down to the mess hall and get some ice."

"Yes, mam."

Brett ran to the mess hall and returned before Marge Thomson had arrived.

Margaret put some ice in a towel and wrapped it around Tim's ankle.

Marge Thomson arrived and examined Tim's ankle. She said, "Obviously, Tim did some damage. I can't believe anything is broken, or he would not have been able to walk on it. If it is a sprain, the ice will help reduce the swelling. However, I would feel better if we had an X-ray to see if there are any fractures. I recommend a trip to the emergency room. In any case, you should get a pair of crutches so Tim doesn't walk or put pressure on the ankle."

Tim said, "Can we eat breakfast first? I've been awake half of the night, and I'm starving."

Marge said, "Yes, you can eat. An hour one way or the other will not matter. However, you must keep ice on it, and you cannot walk on it. I will get my husband and your father. They can carry you to the mess hall on a chair."

After breakfast, Robert and Margaret took Tim to the hospital. Margaret was not happy about riding down the mountain road. She closed her eyes and gripped the armrest until the car leveled off and came to a stop at the paved county road. Robert drove to the library to ask for directions to the hospital. Ms. Linda drew a little road map for Robert to follow. The only hospital in the area was in the town of Cedarville.

Dr. Jason York introduced himself as he entered the examination room. He asked, "What brings you good folks here today?"

Tim said, "I went on a hike yesterday. Last night, I woke up with a sharp pain in my ankle. It's all swollen. I must have twisted my ankle while climbing the rock walls."

Dr. York said, "Let me take a look at your ankle."

Tim pulled up his pant leg and exposed a severely swollen right ankle."

Dr. York gently handled Tim's ankle. He then said, "Let's pull those pants up higher." He then examined Tim's leg all the way up to above the knee.

Dr. York said, "Timothy, let's talk about your hike. Do you remember twisting your ankle?

"Yes."

"Did you fall or limp after twisting your ankle?"

"I did not fall. I just limped a couple of steps. Then it was no problem."

Dr. York said, "Okay. You said you woke up in pain."

"Yes. Sometime in the middle of the night, I woke up from the pain. I couldn't go back to sleep."

Dr. York then looked through a couple of drawers in a medical cabinet and withdrew a magnifying glass. He then turned on an overhead adjustable light and began a very detailed close-up examination of every inch of Tim's foot, ankle, and lower leg.

Addressing Robert and Margaret, Dr. York asked, "Is your son allergic to any medications?"

Robert said, "Nothing to our knowledge."

"What about beestings?"

"Not to our knowledge. I don't remember Tim ever being stung."

Dr. York asked, "Are you folks camping?"

Margaret said, "We are vacationing in an old mountaintop camp. Timothy and his brother are sleeping in a cabin."

Dr. York said, "I think Timothy was bitten by a spider. I think the swelling is an allergic reaction. If Timothy had sprained his ankle, he would have felt some immediate discomfort. It would have been a problem throughout the day. Since Timothy woke up feeling pain, I think he awoke when he was bitten. Look here." Dr. York then handed the magnifying glass to Robert and indicated that he should look closely at a spot on Timothy's foot.

Robert said, "Yeah, the spot is really red."

Robert then handed the magnifying glass to Margaret.

Dr. York said, "It is my opinion that a spider bit Timothy. He has obviously had an allergic reaction. I examined his leg. I don't think there are any problems with blood poisoning. I don't anticipate any complications. However, if for any reason Timothy feels a tightening in his throat, you must bring him back here immediately."

Margaret asked, "Do we need to give him any medications?"

Dr. York said, "No. Maybe a couple of aspirin if he is uncomfortable."

Dr. York said, "Timothy, there's not a lot you can do about spiders or snakes. However, when camping, I suggest you examine your sleeping bag for spiders before you get into bed and examine your shoes or boots before you put them on in the morning. Other than that, enjoy the remainder of your vacation."

Tim said, "Thank you, Doctor. I will check my sleeping bag and shoes, just like you said."

Dr. York said, "You folks enjoy your vacation."

Robert and Margaret both thanked the Doctor.

On the return trip to Cooper's Camp, Tim was quiet.

Margaret said, "Timothy, are you okay? You seem to be quiet."

Tim said, "You know, Mom, Dr. York was pretty good. He listened to me, and he was pretty careful trying to figure out what happened."

Robert said, "Yes, Tim. Dr. York was skillful in his logic and examining skills. He didn't just accept one theory. He allowed the evidence to speak for itself."

Tim said, "Maybe someday I will be a doctor."

Margaret said, "Timothy, we have been blessed to live in a country that will offer you many opportunities to be whatever you desire."

As Robert stopped the car in the designated area prior to driving up the access road, he declared, "It looks clear. Here we go."

Tim said, "Go fast, Dad. Let's see how fast you can climb the mountain."

Margaret said, "Son, you better hush, or you will need that doctor again, and it will not be for your foot."

Robert stepped on the gas just to spin the drive wheels a little.

Margaret asked, "Honey, are you planning to sleep in the boys' cabin tonight?"

Robert and Tim laughed. Margaret closed her eyes and held on.

Robert, Margaret, and Tim found Cooper's Camp to be empty. Apparently, the vacationers had gone someplace. Margaret fixed a light lunch. After lunch, they settled into the rocking chairs on the porch of the main house. Timothy sat in a lounge chair with his foot elevated and wrapped in an ice pack. The three used this time to read.

Tim read three chapters in the Bible. He then read four chapters of *Huckleberry Finn*. Then he began writing in his journal.

Day 4, August 9, 1957

> Day four of our family vacation was exciting. A large group of us went hiking. Brett and me were assigned to Team Thomson. Mr. Thomson is a real leader. He played and coached football. He is now a lawyer. I thought about being a lawyer like Mr. Thomson, but now I think I might be a doctor like Doctor York.
>
> I woke up real early today with a pain in my right foot. I thought I hurt my foot while climbing the rock walls. Mom and Dad took me to the hospital. Dr. York asked me what happened. He then did an examination with a magnifying glass. He found a small spider bite. Apparently, I have some kind of an allergy to spider bites. Dr. York gave me some advice. Check my sleeping bag and shoes for spiders and snakes.
>
> I am getting tired.
>
> Goodbye.
> Overcomer

Tim closed his journal and drifted off into a deep sleep. An hour later, Tim awoke with his mother standing over him. She was holding his arms and was saying, "Timothy, Timothy, are you okay?"

Tim awoke from a disturbing dream. His mother was trying to calm him down.

As Tim began to wake up, he realized that he had been sweating. His mother was trying to wake him and calm him down at the same time.

Margaret kept saying, "It's okay, Timothy. You were just having a dream. It's okay, Timothy."

Tim finally cleared his head and realized what had happened. As he began settling down, he said, "Mom, I have never had a dream like that. I just had a dream that seemed so real. I saw a big flash of light and then darkness. I even had weird smells, and I could feel the rain."

Margaret said, "Timothy, we all have bad dreams once in a while. You had a rough night last night. It's probably just your body being out of routine."

Margaret said, "Robert, please go get a washbasin and a bucket of water. Timothy needs to clean up."

Tim's dream would haunt him for many years to come.

*****

The vacationers returned from their day trip. Everyone enjoyed a dinner of hamburgers, hotdogs, baked beans, and macaroni and cheese. Homemade ice cream was smeared between chocolate chip cookies for the creation of the popular and messy ice cream cookie sandwiches.

Charles Lettice directed the evening activities. The entire group of vacationers was divided into three teams. Each team was given a general theme for the development of a skit. Each team would create three phases for their respective skit. Each skit needed to have an introduction, a main presentation of the theme, and a final conclusion. The skits would be performed on tomorrow's final night of the vacation. This activity was taken as a serious challenge. In the past, some teams would go into town and buy cheap items for costumes or props. As seen in this vacation, the winning team from skit night was excused from all cleanup duties for the next year.

37

Pastor Cooper was normally in attendance during this annual vacation trip, and he always served as the judge. Unfortunately, Pastor Cooper was unable to make the trip this year. Charles Lettice declared himself to be the judge for the skits this year. This announcement brought a resounding *boo* and *hiss*.

Just before everyone turned in for the night, Tim asked if he could make an announcement. With everyone's attention, from his seat, Tim said, "Ladies and gentlemen, take my advice. Check for spiders, and avoid their bites. Check your shoes for snakes to avoid their aches."

Everyone applauded.

CHAPTER 7

The last full day of vacation means the meals are a combination of whatever foods remain to be eaten. Breakfast foods included eggs, pancakes, bacon, sausage, sticky buns, doughnuts, toast, and chocolate chip cookies.

Charles Lettice didn't need to announce any group activity for the day. The last day of vacation allowed for families to do whatever they wished. In addition, skit teams would prepare for the closing skit night. However, as everyone was enjoying breakfast, a car pulled into the parking area. It was unusual to have visitors. Charles was the first to notice the visitor, and he proceeded to investigate the purpose for this visit. Charles approached the lady and introduced himself.

"Good morning. My name is Charles. May I help you?"

"Good morning, Charles. My name is Linda Miller. By the smell of things, maybe you could help me find some bacon."

Charles appreciated the visitor's sense of humor and responded with a bow and said, "My lady, your wish is my command."

Linda smiled and said, "Prince Charles, I have a message from Pastor Cooper to deliver to Timothy Sands and his parents."

Charles responded with a look of concern.

Linda said, "I believe the message will be received as good news."

"No problem. I will get Tim and his parents. I will also make sure your bacon is ready after you deliver the message."

Linda made her way onto the porch overlooking the valley. She sat on her favorite rocking chair and enjoyed the beautiful scenery. Pastor Cooper gave Linda and her husband free access to the camp at times when guests were not scheduled.

Robert, Margaret, and Tim made their way to the main house. Tim was walking slowly. The swelling on his right foot was reduced, but walking caused a little discomfort.

Linda greeted the Sands, but she didn't bother getting up. She said, "This view is a testament to God's creativity. I just love this place. Tim, I thought you would be using crutches."

Margaret said, "Timothy is doing well. Apparently, he had an allergic response to a spider bite."

Linda said, "Pastor Cooper called me late last night. He has a message for Tim that needs to be delivered immediately."

Tim said, "Is it about the wave offering?"

Robert said, "Okay. Somebody needs to tell me what is going on."

Linda said, "Tim, maybe you need to tell your parents why you called Pastor Cooper, and then I can give you his message of response."

Tim hesitated and then said, "I'm not supposed to talk about this."

Margaret said, "Tim, does this have anything to do with Brett's adoption?"

Tim said, "Yes."

Robert said, "Tim, what's this all about? Tell me, now."

Tim said, "Brett told me Mr. and Mrs. Corson were trying to adopt him, but they can't, because they are short five thousand dollars."

Robert said, "Keep going. Why did you call Pastor Cooper?"

Tim said, "I know God is going to give the Corsons the money, so I asked Pastor Cooper to have a wave offering on Sunday."

Linda said, "Mr. Sands, can I tell you why Pastor Cooper called?"
"Please do."

Linda said, "Pastor Cooper said he was struggling with what to do with Tim's request. He wasn't sure the wave offering was the best way to deal with the adoption problem. He couldn't get past Tim's assurance that God was going to provide. Yesterday, he had a couple visit his office. The couple wished to remain anonymous. The couple had an unexpected death in the family. As a result of the death, the couple inherited a good amount of money from an insurance policy on the deceased. The couple wanted to make a donation to the church. Pastor Cooper felt that he had to explain an immediate need for a Christian family to adopt a young boy. The couple was completely in support of directing their donation to finalize the adoption. The couple gave Pastor Cooper an envelope with five thousand dollars' cash. Pastor Cooper's message to Timothy is 'God provided according to your faith. When you get home, come pick up the adoption money for Brett Young.' Pastor Cooper called me with this message late yesterday afternoon. I had to wait until this morning because I will not drive up that access road at night."

Robert said, "Wow! That is some story."

Tim said, "I knew God was going to do it, and he worked really fast. Maybe he knew the Corsons needed it now."

Margaret had tears running down her cheeks.

Linda said, "A Mr. Prince Charles said he was going to save me some breakfast."

Robert said, "Linda, come with me up to the mess hall. I will hook you up with Charles, and then I will bring the Corsons and Brett back here. We can share the news with the Corsons."

Linda got up from her rocking chair and walked with Robert toward the mess hall.

Robert introduced Linda to the vacationers. Charles served her with a breakfast dish, which was heavy on the bacon. As Linda was enjoying breakfast and talking with various vacationers, she observed the two families on the front porch of the main house, hugging. She smiled and whispered, "Thank you, Lord, for answering that young boy's prayer."

The Corson's and the Sands returned to the mess hall. David Corson asked if he could have everyone's attention. David said, "My dear friends, Lisa and I have been working on a plan to adopt Brett Young. We were unable to complete the process, because we didn't have enough money. We—no—I thought the best way to proceed was to not tell anyone. I was wrong in not telling you, our friends. I apologize for not telling you of our plans and of our needs. I hope you will forgive me. We are happy to tell you that we just found out

41

that we can proceed with the adoption of Brett." Everyone broke into a cheer and applause.

Brett said, "This vacation has been the greatest ever. I now have a family. I now have a new best friend. Ms. Linda helped me overcome a reading problem. I also found out that God does answer prayer."

Charles led the group in a loud *hurrah*.

Breakfast at Cooper's Camp ended on a high level of joy. Linda wanted to speak with Tim and Brett before she left. Linda said, "I have been a schoolteacher and a librarian for many years. I have never been so impressed with two young men as I have with both of you. Tim, when you came to the library to buy some used books, you asked about purchasing a journal for Brett. I didn't have any journals for purchase. After you both left, I felt it was important that Brett should have a journal. Therefore, I purchased one and now give it to you as a gift." Linda handed Brett a soft-leather-bound journal.

Linda said, "For some reason, I didn't get your name embossed on the cover of your journal. Now I understand why. After your adoption is final, you can take your journal and have your new name inscribed on the book."

Brett gave Ms. Linda a hug. He said, "Thank you. I have a lot of things to write in my journal."

*****

Tim and Brett sat together on Tim's lower bunk bed for observance of the daily quiet time. After Tim's encounter with a spider, Tim and Brett exchanged bunks. Brett moved up, and Tim moved down.

The two friends talked. They were so excited about the events of yesterday and today that they didn't even read from the Bible or from their respective books. They did want to write something in their journals. They decided to write the same thing in each book.

However, they wanted to write a list of things they enjoyed about this vacation. They agreed on the following:

Last day of vacation—August 10, 1957

The following is a list of things Tim and Brett enjoyed while on vacation at Cooper's Camp:

1. Country: We live in a great country. We raised the flag. We thank God for freedom and liberty, and we honor those who defend our freedoms.
2. Family: We have great families and friends. It is fun having vacations with family friends at Cooper's Camp.
3. Faith: We found out that God answers our prayers. We found out that God knows what will happen because he is in charge.
4. Books: We found out that reading is fun. We can travel into the past or future with book stories.
5. Friends: We have friends because we are friends.
6. Leaders: We see leaders (Dad, Mom, Pastor Cooper, Charles Lettice, Richard Thomson, Ms. Linda) and want to be leaders like them.

Vacation this year has been great.

Goodbye.
Overcomer

CHAPTER 8

The vacationers packed their cars and closed down Cooper's Camp. It was a rainy day, and Margaret was not looking forward to riding down the access road in these conditions.

Margaret said, "Robert, what can you do if the car begins slipping on the wet road?"

Robert said, "Relax. Everything will be fine."

Charles Lettice was driving the lead car. Robert Sands fell into the tail end of the caravan. Just after the hairpin turn, Charles's car began to skid and slid off to the mountainside of the road. That was certainly less dangerous than sliding off the cliffside of the road. The drivers following Charles all needed to apply their brakes. The situation became a problem because some cars continued to slide on the wet road even with the wheels completely locked up.

When all of the cars were stopped, the men all gathered around Charles's car and successfully pushed the car out of a small ditch on the mountainside of the road. Tragedy was averted, and everyone safely descended the access road.

Margaret proclaimed, "I will never, ever drive up or down that road again when it is wet."

John said, "Mom, you never drive up or down the access road. Dad always does the driving."

Margaret said, "You know what I mean. End of discussion."

When Margaret used the phrase "end of discussion," everyone in the family knew she was upset and they better not continue any further discussion on the subject at hand.

Part 2

The Adventures
of a Teenager

I may not have gone where I intended to go, but I
think I have ended up where I intended to be.

—Douglas Adams

CHAPTER 9

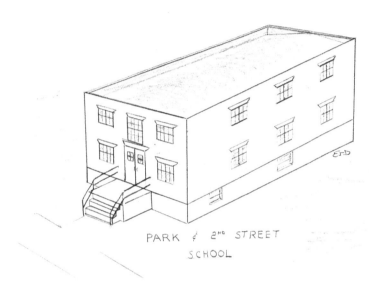

PARK & 2ᴺᴰ STREET
SCHOOL

Summer had come to an end. Timothy was a good student, and he was looking forward to the start of a new school year. He was excited about being assigned to the old Park and Second Street School. This school was an old two-room building. The fifth-grade class was assigned to the first floor, and the sixth grade was assigned to the upper classroom. Music lessons were held in the unfinished basement. Tim would be starting the fifth grade. The Park and Second Street School was about twice as far away from Tim's home than his previous school but was still within walking distance.

Most of the students in the fifth- and sixth-grade classes were friends. They all lived in the same neighborhood and had been classmates throughout the years. The only new person in the fifth-grade class at the Park and Second Street School was the teacher. Ms. Abbey Beachum introduced herself as excited to be teaching for the first time. Ms. Beachum tried to be upbeat and positive, but she seemed to be rule orientated. She also seemed to be preoccupied with trying to make everyone like her. Unfortunately, she was quick to identify favorite students. By the end of day one, the students in the fifth grade of Park and Second Street School labeled their new teacher as Ms. Crabby something.

Margaret Sands was anxious to hear from her children about the first day of the new school year. John was starting his first year in a new high school. Sandra was in seventh grade at the junior high school. Timothy was attending the old Park and Second Street School. John and Sandra had both attended the old two-room school.

During dinner, Margaret said, "I'm anxious to hear about your new schools. John, what is the new high school like?"

John said, "The building is huge. At first, it was kind of hard to get around. It got easier as the day went on. My classes are okay."

Sandra said, "I heard John has a girlfriend."

"Mind your own business, bigmouth."

Robert said, "John, don't be rude."

Margaret said, "John, the school seems like it is big. Do you know how many students are in your class?"

John said, "I have no clue."

Robert said, "I read in the newspaper the new high school was designed for over three thousand students."

John said, "Yeah, I think I ran into a thousand students in the hallways. It's like a slow-moving mob when you change classes."

Margaret said, "And the girlfriend?"

John said, "It's no big deal. I have a friend that has my same schedule. I offered to carry her books."

"Does she have a name?"

John said, "I think so."

Margaret said, "Okay, for now. However, I fully expect you to talk to your father and me if you get beyond carrying books for a classmate."

Robert said, "Sandra, how was your first day in middle school? Did anyone offer to carry your books?"

Sandra said, "No. All the boys in my class are morons. I would burn my books if any of those creeps touch them."

Margaret said, "Okay, let's get back on track. How was your first day in middle school?"

"It was fine. I like my classes and my teachers. It's fun moving from class to class. I think I will like my science teacher the best."

Margaret asked, "Timothy, how do you like the old Park and Second Street School?"

Tim said, "The school is great. My teacher is a new teacher. Her name is Ms. Abbey Beachum. By lunchtime, she was being called Ms. Crabby something."

Sandra said, "Say it, Timmy. Say her last name. I dare you."

Margaret said, "Sandra, you seem to know a lot about everything in different schools besides your own."

Sandra said, "I have friends in high school and in the old Park and Second Street School. Timmy's class hates the new teacher. Except for her two pet students."

Margaret said, "Timothy, I don't expect you to be calling your teacher bad names. If she is a new teacher, you can't judge her by just her first day."

Tim said, "I didn't call her bad names. I don't like the way she talks down to some students. I hope tomorrow is better."

Robert said, "Tim, you have always been a good student. Just do your best. I do want you to talk with us if something happens to be upsetting. Okay?"

"I will."

CHAPTER 10

Day two in fifth grade at the Park and Second Street School started with new seating assignments. Ms. Beachum had the entire class take a test in English, math, science, and social studies. She said, "Testing was necessary to know the various levels of learning among the class. The results of the testing would determine future seating assignments."

At the end of the day, Ms. Beachum gave a homework assignment.

Ms. Beachum said, "Tomorrow, everyone will give an oral report on something factual that happened over the summer."

On the following day, Ms. Beachum said, "Class, everyone needs to read this morning because I didn't have enough time to grade all the tests from yesterday. I was up until ten o'clock last night. Read or put your heads down on your desk."

Sara raised her hand.

Ms. Beachum said, "Yes, Sara."

Sara said, "What do you want us to read?"

Ms. Beachum said, "Now, Sara, I said you should read. I didn't specify any particular book. On the first day of school, I gave you an English book and a science book and social studies book. You can read whatever you want."

After lunch, Ms. Beachum called upon students to give their oral reports. The process was troubling. Ms. Beachum was openly critical of the reports, except for her pet students.

Ms. Beachum called upon Timothy Sands.

Tim stood in front of the class and opened his leather-bound journal. He shared the six points he had written in his journal on the last day of his vacation.

Ms. Beachum said, "Timothy Sands, that presentation has earned an F. I asked for a factual report. You spoke in generalities and of friends and faith, which can't be proven to be factual. Even your reference to reading books was referring to fiction. Please give me the book from which you were reading."

Timothy handed Miss Beachum his journal. She took his journal and turned to the page Tim had marked with the string marker. She saw the six points he had referenced in his report. She took her red pen and marked the page with an F. She then recorded an F in her grade book for Timothy's oral report. She handed him back his book and said, "Please take your seat."

Timothy was very quiet at dinner that night. He didn't say much and went to his bedroom early.

Margaret sensed something was wrong. Later in the evening, she knocked on Timothy's door. Tim knew it was his mother. He could tell by the sound of her walking down the hall.

"Come in, Mom."

Margaret sat down on his bed but didn't say anything.

Tim said, "I had a bad day in school today."

"How bad?"

"Bad enough to get an F on an assignment."

"Timothy, that is certainly not typical of your grades. What happened?"

"Ms. Beachum said I didn't follow her instructions."

Margaret said, "Is this something I need to get involved with?"

Tim said, "No. It's just one assignment grade. It will not happen again."

Margaret sat for a while and then said, "Something else besides the F is bothering you. What is it?"

"The teacher pronounced the failing grade to the entire class."

Margaret said, "Timothy, I'm so sorry you were publicly embarrassed. That should have never happened. I will make an appointment to talk with your teacher."

Tim said, "No, Mom. I will deal with this."

Margaret said, "Okay. I will not push this, but I will talk to your father. As long as he is in agreement, we will not get involved in this assignment. However, if something like this happens again, we will deal with it as a family. Understand?"

"Yes, Mom. Thank you."

Margaret kissed Timothy on the forehead and closed the door behind her as she left.

Tim sat on his bed looking at his journal for a long time. He began to evaluate his journal entries. He thought, *These comments are factual.* He turned to his dictionary and looked up the word *factual.* The definition of *factual* was "concerning with what is actually the case rather than interpretations or reactions to it." Tim went to his desk and began writing in his journal.

September 8, 1957

> I commit to living my life to prove the following:

1. I live in a great country. I will thank God for our freedom and liberties. I will honor those who defend our freedoms. I will raise the American flag.
2. I have a great family. I will raise a great family.
3. I will have faith in God.
4. I will encourage reading all kinds of books.
5. I will have friends, and I will be a friend.
6. I will be a leader.

> Lord, I need you to help me with my teacher. I don't know what to do, but I have faith that you will help me.
>
> Goodbye
>
> Overcomer—How can I overcome a problem outside of my control?

Tim was committed to being a good student. He struggled with his teacher but did the best he could to maintain good grades. Some of the students began to be rebellious, and at times, the classroom was an unpleasant place to be.

During the Christmas break, Robert and Margaret Sands received a letter from the local school board. The letter advised the parents of all fifth-grade students at the Park and Second Street School that Ms. Abbey Beachum would no longer be the teacher for this class. The school board has determined that Mrs. Georgeann Costello will be assigned to this class upon return from the Christmas break. The school board anticipates a smooth transition of leadership in this class.

Robert and Margaret shared the letter from the school board with Timothy.

Tim simply said, "Mom and Dad, I have a question. Why does God sometimes answer our prayers quickly and then at other times he is slow to react?"

Robert said, "Tim, are you saying you prayed for Ms. Beachum to be replaced?"

Tim said, "Not really. I asked God to help me deal with her. But it wasn't working out really well. For some of my classmates, things have gotten really bad."

Margaret said, "Timothy, apparently the school board felt that Ms. Beachum was not the right teacher for your class. Maybe Ms. Beachum realized that teaching was not her calling. Either way, you tried to do your best in a difficult situation. Maybe your prayer was answered in how you adjusted."

Tim said, "Yeah, I did make a commitment to prove something."

CHAPTER 11

The remainder of the school year was a wholesome and encouraging learning experience under the teaching of Mrs. Georgeann Costello. However, Tim's class and the entire community experienced a tragic event on the last day of school. One of Tim's classmates disappeared. The circumstances surrounding Mindy Young's disappearance were disturbing and resulted in no clues or witnesses. The police were able to determine that Mindy stayed after school for just a few minutes while talking to her teacher. This delay resulted in Mindy walking home by herself. The distance from the school to Mindy's home was only about one mile. The police interviewed homeowners and residents along the route from school to Mindy's home, and no one reported seeing anything.

Tim began the summer by looking for a job. He asked his parents if he could either begin delivering newspapers or possibly cutting grass for neighbors. Tim was interested in earning some spending money.

Robert and Margaret had allowed John to earn spending money through summer part-time jobs. Sandra had earned spending money by babysitting. However, with the recent disappearance of Mindy Young, Tim's parents were concerned about having Tim roaming the neighborhood by himself. They had a long conversation and agreed that Tim could cut lawns if he would abide by their warnings.

Robert said, "Tim, your mother and I have come to a decision to allow you to cut lawns to earn some spending money. However, in light of Mindy Young's disappearance, you must abide by our restrictions."

"Okay, what do I need to do?"

Margaret said, "Timothy, you must tell me where you are going each day. You can only cut a lawn if the homeowner is home. If any stranger approaches you, immediately go directly to the homeowner and report this activity."

Tim said, "I understand. I'll be careful."

Tim began his summer vacation by playing baseball and cutting grass. On Tim's first day of cutting grass, he was able to secure two customers. He cut the grass for the Coulter and Logan families. While walking home from these two jobs, Tim noticed that the Young family's grass needed to be cut. He was a little nervous about talking to Mindy's parents. He wasn't sure what he should say.

Tim knocked on the door.

Mrs. Young opened the door and said, "Hello, Timothy."

Tim said, "Mrs. Young, I noticed your lawn needs to be cut. May I cut your grass?"

Mrs. Young said, "Timothy, I know our lawn needs to be cut. We just haven't paid any attention to things like that."

Tim said, "I don't want any money. I just want to help you."

Mrs. Young replied, "Timothy, that's very kind of you. Please go ahead and cut the lawn. We will gladly pay you for your work."

Tim said, "Please, Mrs. Young, I don't want any money from you."

Mrs. Young said, "Timothy, I understand. Thank you for your kindness."

That night, at the dinner table, Margaret asked Timothy how his part-time job was coming along.

Tim said, "I cut grass for three families. The Coulters, Logans, and the Youngs."

Margaret said, "Timothy, I received a phone call from Mrs. Young. She was very impressed with your desire to help them. She told me you would not take any money for cutting their lawn."

Tim said, "I didn't care about the money. I was just afraid to talk to Mindy's mother. I wanted to help them, but I didn't know how to talk about Mindy."

"Timothy, sometimes, we don't need to say anything when others are hurting. You did the right thing."

CHAPTER 12

Tim's second and third days of cutting grass were successful. He was earning ten dollars per cut. He already had his eye on a new baseball glove he wanted to buy and was also hoping to buy a new bicycle.

Tim approached the house of someone he did not know. A man was sitting in a wheelchair on his front porch.

Tim said, "Sir, would you like to have me cut your grass? I only charge ten dollars."

The man said, "Ten dollars sounds like a fair price. Go ahead and cut the grass."

Tim began cutting the grass, but he noticed the man got up from the wheelchair and walked into the house. A few minutes later, the man returned and sat back down on the wheelchair. While Tim was cutting the grass on the side of the house, something moved behind a basement window. Tim wasn't sure what caught his attention. Was it a cat or a curtain or just his own reflection on the glass? As Tim thought about the movement, it appeared like someone was rubbing a broom against the glass. Tim thought maybe the man's wife was cleaning the basement.

While Tim was finishing cutting the grass, something started to bother him. If the man had a wife, how come Tim never saw her sitting on the porch? In fact, Tim noticed that no other chairs were on the porch. Tim wondered why the man was sitting on a wheelchair when he could walk? Something wasn't right.

Tim finished the job by sweeping off the grass cuttings from the sidewalk. He then announced to the man that he was done.

The man said, "You did a fine job. I owe you ten dollars." The man began moving his wheelchair toward the door. He then said,

"Young man, why don't you come up here on the porch? You can hold open the door for me."

Tim did not like the idea that the man was using his wheelchair to get him to hold open the door. Tim knew the man was able to walk. Why was he trying to get Tim to hold open the door?

Tim said, "Mister, I'm running late. My mother will be mad if I don't get home right now."

The man said, "It will only take a minute to get your money. It will be quicker if you come in."

Tim began walking away while pushing his mower. Tim said, "I need to get home."

The man said something, but Tim was unable to hear what was said over the sound of the mower wheels rumbling down the sidewalk.

Tim was happy that Brett was going to stay over for the weekend. After dinner, Tim and Brett sat outside on the back porch steps. Brett could tell something was on Tim's mind.

"Tim, what's up? You seem to be bothered about something."

Tim told Brett about his encounter with the man in the wheelchair. Tim said, "Something about that basement window is bothering me. I don't know if it was just my imagination or a reflection or just a cat, but something drew my attention to that window. Let's go over to that house and look in the window."

"Are you crazy? We can't just go peeking in someone's window."

Tim's brother, John, was walking out the back door when he heard Brett say something about Tim being crazy.

John said, "Good observation, Brett. Timmy is crazy."

Brett said, "I didn't say Tim was crazy. I said what he wants to do is crazy."

John said, "So what crazy thing does my crazy brother want to do?"

Tim said, "You know the big white house on West Avenue where the old man often sits on the porch in a wheelchair?"

John said, "Yeah. So a man sits in a wheelchair. Big deal."

Tim said, "Yes, but the man can walk."

John said, "So what?"

Tim said, "He tried to get me to go into his house."

John said, "So did you?"

Tim said, "No."

John said, "So what do you want to do?"

Tim said, "When I was cutting his grass, I saw something in his basement window."

John said, "What did you see?"

"I'm not sure. It could have been my reflection or a cat or a broom."

John said, "Brett is right—you are crazy. You saw something, but you're not sure what you saw. So you want to go peeping into some guy's window. You better be careful. That old man might just call the cops on you."

John's friends pulled into the driveway. As John was getting into his friend's car, he said, "Dad won't be happy if he gets a call from the police to come bail you out of jail."

Tim said to Brett, "I'm going to go. Are you in or out?"

Brett said, "You know I'm in."

Tim ran into the house to get a flashlight.

Tim and Brett began their adventure by sneaking through some backyards to approach the big white house from the back. The two boys began crawling along the foundation of the house to reach the basement window. The basement was dark. No light was shining in the basement. Tim and Brett cupped their hands around their face and pressed up against the window. They couldn't see anything. Tim turned on the flashlight. The two boys looked into the window. It took a few seconds to discern what they were seeing.

Tim started to say, "What the heck…"

Suddenly, the homeowner grabbed the two boys by the back of their necks. The man was strong and held a firm grip with one hand on each boy. The man said, "You boys just made a big mistake."

The boys tried to fight against the man's grip, but they were no matches for his strength, and he was not letting up on his grip. He started to drag the two boys into his house. At that moment, a car, which was parked down the street, was started; and its lights were turned on, and the driver drove the car onto the man's front yard.

Immediately, three teenagers jumped out of the car and confronted the man.

John said, "Mister, you better let go of my brother and his friend."

The man said, "Get out of my yard. I'm calling the cops on you for trespassing."

Tim tried his best to yell, "John, call the police. Mindy is in his basement."

The man started choking Tim to shut him up.

One of John's friends, Joe Hazel, is the biggest and strongest player on the high school football team. Joe said, "Mister, if you hurt Mindy, you are going to regret what you did." Joe then proceeded to run at full speed and drove his shoulder into the man's unprotected chest and tackled the man so hard it knocked the wind out of the man. In the brief moment in which the man was trying to catch his breath, he released his grip on Tim and Brett, and all five teenagers piled on him. Joe then proceeded to hold the man in a firm headlock.

John yelled to Tim, "Go to the house next door, and call the police."

In a matter of minutes, the police arrived. The man was arrested; medical teams began providing assistance to Mindy Young and another girl. The two girls were found bound by chains. They were starving and dehydrated, and they were abused in unimaginable ways.

Tim went back to the next-door neighbor's house and called his parents. He briefly told his mother what happened. He said, "Mom, you and Dad need to go and get Mindy's parents and bring them over here right now."

The local and national newspapers reported on the kidnapping, torture, and rescue of the two young girls, Mindy Young and Linda Cassidy. The man responsible for this horrible crime was being held without bail on kidnapping, torture, rape, slavery, and other appropriate charges. The police began searching cold cases in other cities and states in which the man may have previously committed similar crimes.

Chapter 13

A couple of weeks after Mindy's rescue, Robert, Margaret, and Timothy Sands were invited to the Youngs' home. Mindy and her parents, Tyrus and Emily Young, wanted to talk to Timothy. At first, Tim didn't want to go. He didn't know what to say. Finally, they all agreed to respond to the invitation.

Robert Sands knocked on the door.

Tyrus Young opened the door and said, "Welcome, my friends. Please come in."

Tyrus shook hands with Robert, Margaret, and Timothy. Emily gave everyone a hug. Mindy was not part of the greeting party.

Emily invited everyone into the living room and offered seats.

Emily said, "We invited you all here for two main reasons. First, to thank you for all that you did to rescue our Mindy. Timothy, we don't know why or how you did what you did, but we are eternally grateful to you. The second reason we invited you over is that Mindy wants to talk to Timothy."

Margaret said, "Emily, how is Mindy doing?"

Emily wiped a tear. "Not very well. We think she is going to need a lot of support for a long time. Mindy was hurt badly, but the other girl was held in captivity much longer. Her future looks grim."

Tim said, "How can I help Mindy?"

Emily said, "Timothy, would you mind meeting with Mindy alone? She does not want to talk to anyone else."

Tim said, "Yes."

Emily escorted Tim to Mindy's room. The door was shut. Emily knocked and said, "Mindy, Timothy Sands is here. Can he come in?"

Mindy said, "Yes."

Emily opened the door. Tim walked in, and Emily shut the door.

Mindy was seated and facing away from Tim.

She said, "Tim, thanks for coming over. Please sit down."

Tim sat in a chair that seemed to be placed in a position for him to see. Tim said, "How are you doing, Mindy?"

Mindy said, "Not very good. Tim, do you mind if I face you?"

Tim said, "Sure. I came here to see you."

Mindy turned to face him.

Tim was shocked at her appearance, but he tried not to react. Mindy's face was swollen, her eye sockets were all black and blue, and she was almost unrecognizable.

Mindy said, "I'm pretty messed up."

Tim said, "Yeah, but you will get better."

"Problem is, I'm messed up in my head worse than my face and body."

Tim said, "How can I help you get better?"

Mindy said, "Are you kidding? You helped me by saving my life."

After a few minutes of silence, Mindy said, "Tim, can I give you a hug?"

Tim got up from his seat, walked over to Mindy, and offered his hand. She took his hand and stood up, and the two friends hugged each other.

Mindy said, "Thank you."

Tim asked, "Can we sit and talk a little longer?"

The two sat together on the edge of her bed.

Tim said, "My mother gave me a journal. I write things in my journal almost every night. Do you have a journal?"

Mindy said, "No."

Tim said, "Okay, I will get you a journal. I want you to write down things that help you get better every day. Write good things. Write down your improvements each day, even just little things. I want you to sign your journal entries with the same title I use for myself."

Mindy said, "What is the title you use?"

Tim looked around Mindy's room and saw her Bible. Tim picked up her Bible and turned to the Revelation 2:17: "To him that overcometh will I give to eat of the hidden manna, and will give him a white stone, and in the stone a new name written, which no man knoweth except he that receiveth it."

Tim said, "I use the name *Overcomer*. That's what you need to be. I know you had a lot of bad things happen to you, but you will be an overcomer."

The two friends sat together for a long time.

Mindy said, "When I saw you cutting the grass, I tried to scream, but I couldn't because of the duct tape over my mouth. I also couldn't get to the window because of the chains."

Tim said, "Did you wipe the glass with a broom?"

Mindy said, "Yes, I tried to smash the glass, but I was too weak."

Tim said, "You did what you could at the time. That's what you need to do now. Do what you can to get better. You will overcome it."

After a few more minutes of silence, Mindy said, "I need another hug."

The two friends hugged.

The next day, Tim purchased a journal for Mindy.

Two weeks later, Emily Young called Margaret Sands.

Emily said, "Margaret, I don't know what Timothy said to Mindy on the day of his visit. However, Mindy has shown steady improvement every day since. Please tell Timothy and thank him for all that he said and did."

Margaret said, "I will. I am so glad Mindy is doing better. I can tell by the sound in your voice that you are doing better as well."

"Yes. I am doing better because Mindy is improving. Thank you."

On the first day of the new school year, Tim knocked on the door of Mindy's home.

Emily Young opened the door and said, "Good morning, Timothy. What can I do for you?"

Tim said, "I just wanted to see if Mindy could walk to school with me?"

Emily said, "Timothy, I think we will drive Mindy to school for a while."

Tim replied, "Okay. I understand."

Emily closed the door. Tim turned away and began walking to school alone. When Tim had walked about three houses down the street, he heard someone calling his name. It was Mindy.

"Tim. Tim. Wait for me."

Tim stopped walking until Mindy caught up to him.

Tim said, "Wow! You look a lot better than you did the last time I saw you."

Mindy smiled.

Tim took Mindy by the hand and led the way by walking to school down a street, which did not pass the big old white house.

Everyone on the school playground welcomed Mindy.

Mrs. Pat Miller was the sixth-grade teacher. She began the first day of class by asking if anyone wanted to share something they learned over the summer. To everyone's surprise, Mindy was the first student to raise her hand.

Mrs. Miller said, "Mindy, if you feel comfortable, please share what you have learned over the summer."

Mindy stood up and walked, with confidence, to the front of the classroom. Mindy said, "This summer, I experienced the highest level of evil in the world. I was hurt physically and mentally in many ways. However, I also experienced the greatest good in the world by you, my friends and my family. I choose to have good to overcome evil in my life."

The entire class jumped to their feet and applauded and shouted with cheers. Mrs. Miller gave Mindy a hug while wiping tears from her face.

CHAPTER 14

During the summer leading up to the start of high school, Tim and Brett set some goals. They certainly wanted to maintain the highest possible grade point average during their four years in high school. Neither expected to be top in their class of almost nine hundred students. They would be happy to graduate in the top 10 percent of their class. However, they both had full expectations of playing varsity level football and baseball.

Another high school objective, which became a larger group goal, was to choose German to fulfill their foreign language academic requirement. If they took four years of this foreign language, they would be eligible to take a club trip to Germany. Tim and Brett shared this objective with friends Mindy Young and Rachel Bennett. The four friends were determined to share in a possible adventure of a club trip to Germany during their senior year of high school.

Following the junior year of high school, Tim, Brett, Mindy, and Rachel each began saving money for their anticipated club trip to Germany. Tim found a summer job of working in a delicatessen. Brett was able to work as a laborer with a construction company. Mindy began working in a grocery store. Rachel began working in an office with a large insurance company.

Tim enjoyed learning about the large variety of foods while working in an Italian deli. Tim also learned what it meant to serve and satisfy his customers. Working in a deli had specific benefits of which Tim took full advantage. On Saturdays, the deli was extremely busy. The owner allowed his workers to make a free lunch if the worker would just eat and go immediately back to work.

Throughout Tim's summer job experience, he became particularly sensitive to certain customers. One gentleman and his wife became Tim's specific regular customers. The other deli clerks did not like to serve this particular customer, because he was very hard to understand. Apparently, the gentleman had some kind of speech impediment. The man stuttered a lot. If he was challenged or misunderstood, he would become upset; and his stuttering would increase, making it even harder to understand him. Tim learned to listen closely to the gentleman. The customer and his wife would patiently wait until Tim was available to serve them.

Late into the summer, Rachel Bennett called Tim while he was working at the deli. One of the clerks answered the phone.

The clerk said, "Tim, you have a phone call." He then set the phone down on the counter.

Tim picked up the phone and said, "Hello."

"Hi, Tim, it's Rachel. Can you do me a favor?"

"Sure. What's up?"

Rachel said, "My aunt and uncle's car broke down, and it's in the repair shop. They wanted me to get them some groceries. I don't have anyone to drive me to your store. Can you fill an order for me?"

Tim said, "Sure. No problem. When I get done with work, I can bring the groceries to your house."

Rachel said, "Great. Thanks."

Rachel then gave Tim the list of groceries.

When Tim finished work, he filled Rachel's grocery list and paid for the items. When Tim arrived at Rachel's house, he saw her sitting on the front step. She jumped up and ran to the curbside.

Tim said, "Jump in. We can take these groceries to your aunt and uncle."

Rachel said, "Thanks, Tim."

She then opened the door and slid into the front seat of Tim's '55 Chevy.

Tim asked, "Where are we going?"

Rachel said, "Head over to West Avenue and Oak Road. I will show you where from there."

As they were heading over to West Avenue, Rachel said, "Tim, just for your information, my uncle has Parkinson's disease."

Tim asked, "Is it contagious?"

"No. It's not contagious. It's a nerve disease."

When Tim arrived at the home, which Rachel had identified, Rachel said, "Tim, please come in with me. I would like you to meet my aunt and uncle."

Rachel knocked but didn't wait for any reply. She opened the door and announced her presence, by saying, "Hello." Rachel took Tim's hand and walked him into the kitchen. Rachel was ready to introduce Tim when her uncle recognized the young man.

Uncle Tony jumped to his feet and bypassed Rachel to welcome Tim with a *"Benvenuto, amico mio."*

Rachel looked at her aunt in surprise.

Aunt Mary said, "Tony said, 'Welcome, my friend.'"

Tony then said, *"Unisciti a me con il vino."*

Aunt Mary said, "Tony, talk in English."

Tony began stuttering, "My friend...share...a glass of wine... with me."

Rachel quickly found herself standing alone as Uncle Tony ushered Tim to the kitchen table and began pouring two glasses of wine.

Rachel said, "Can someone tell me what just happened?"

Aunt Mary took the groceries from Rachel's hand and said, "Your friend is our clerk at Mario's Deli. He is the only clerk your uncle Tony will deal with."

Tim had never even tasted wine. He said, "Please, only just a little wine. I'm driving."

Aunt Mary said something to Tony in Italian.

He nodded and said, "Yes, dear." He then produced four glasses. Two full glasses. He gave one to Mary and kept one for himself. He then poured a small amount in two glasses. He gave one to Tim and one to Rachel.

Uncle Tony held up his glass and said, "Salute, *cent anno.*"

Aunt Mary said, "He said, 'Well-being for one hundred years.'"

The four clinked their glasses.

As Tim was driving Rachel home, she said, "Tim, you really made a big impression on my aunt and uncle."

Tim said, "They made a big impression on me."

Rachel asked, "How?"

Tim said, "They have learned to live life to the fullest, even with a disability. Your uncle Tony wished us with well-being for one hundred years. That's cool."

CHAPTER 15

The final arrangements were made for the high school German Club to travel to Germany. After the final agenda was published, Tim, Brett, and Rachel were invited to Mindy's home to discuss the trip to Germany.

Mindy greeted her friends at the front door. However, she did not seem to be very happy.

Mindy said, "Thanks for coming over. My parents want to talk to you guys."

Emily Young greeted Mindy's friends. She invited them all to the living room. Mr. Young was seated, but he stood up to greet the teens.

After everyone was seated, Emily said, "We wanted to talk to all of you at the same time. When we received the agenda for your club trip to Germany, we felt it would be best if Mindy did not go. It appears that the club is planning to visit the Dachau Concentration Camp in Munich, Germany. Given Mindy's previous experiences, we do not want her exposed to the horrors of such a place."

Rachel said, "Mrs. Young, I understand your concerns. However, if we can get our teacher to change the agenda, will you still allow Mindy to go?"

Tyrus Young said, "Rachel, we think the entire club should have the experience of seeing the Dachau concentration camp. You should all have a true account of the history associated with this tragedy. However, this is just not something we want for Mindy, given her own real-life tragedy."

Tim said, "Mr. Young, my mother is traveling on this trip as a chaperone. If I could get our teacher to allow my mother and Mindy to skip that one stop on the agenda. Would you reconsider?"

Tyrus looked at his wife with a questioning look. She nodded with a yes. Tyrus said, "Timothy, I think your proposal is worth exploring."

Mindy's face turned from a sullen frown to a full blown beaming smile. She simply said, "Yes."

Tim said, "I will talk to my mother. I'm sure she will talk to Mrs. Schmidt."

Brett said, "Mrs. Young, I thought you invited us all here for pizza."

Everyone laughed.

Tyrus Young said, "You guys go play some board games. I will order some pizza."

There was a collective "Yes."

Chapter 16

Mrs. Schmidt addressed the twenty students and five chaperones concerning the rules and expectations for good behavior while on the trip to Germany. Mrs. Schmidt also reviewed the agenda and reinforced the expectation that each student is expected to choose one aspect of the trip and develop a written report on that topic. The agenda included the following:

- Day 1: Stuttgart—arrival location—one-night stay and start of the bus trip
- Day 2 and 3: Munich—two nights' stay—one-day walking tour of the city and one-day tour of the Dachau Concentration Camp
- Day 4 and 5: Heidelberg—two-day walking tour—two-night stay
- Day 6: Linderhof Palace—one-day walking tour
- Day 7: Schwaebisch Hall—one-night stay
- Day 8: Stuttgart—departure location

Mrs. Schmidt said, "I also want to remind everyone, if you purchase gifts, they must fit inside your luggage for the return flight. I would like for everyone to interact with the people in their native language as much as possible. However, you should not be surprised if the German people will want to talk to you in English. Just like we are trying to practice our use of German, they are trying to practice their English. Have fun with your interaction with the German people."

The first day of touring the city of Munich set a fast pace of trying to see everything and eating as much as possible. It quickly became clear that a one-day tour was only going to allow for a glimpse of its history, architecture, and art. One historic marketplace dated back its establishment to 1823. One museum displayed original Renaissance and Baroque paintings, pottery, and religious items. Everyone enjoyed the apple strudel at a Bavarian Coffeehouse.

Margaret Sands and Mindy Young did not participate in the next day's visit to Dachau Concentration Camp. Mrs. Schmidt made arrangements for Margaret and Mindy to visit with a librarian and a historian for a private tour of the Marienplatz Square clock tower and the famous half-timbered town hall.

Tim, Brett, and Rachel stayed together as they toured the Dachau Concentration Camp. As the three friends entered the camp by walking over the railroad tracks and through an open iron gate with barbed wire fencing, Tim commented, "Can you feel the atmosphere of heaviness and oppression?"

Rachel said, "Yes. This place is creepy."

The three friends began their tour by walking through the historical museum. The museum had enlarged photos of persons in deep distress. Some stations described horrendous experiments conducted on people. Photos and descriptions of the gas chambers, ovens, and mass graves began to have an effect on Rachel. After a short time, Rachel said, "I'm glad Mindy is not seeing this stuff."

Tim and Brett both agreed with a nod.

As the three friends exited the museum, they found themselves standing in the main portion of the camp. One building remained as a sample of the housing for the prisoners. The building was a wooded-style barracks with triple bunk beds with maybe two feet between the beds. The photos showed how horrible these living conditions were at the time. Only the foundations of all of the other thirty-one barracks were still visible. This image made an impact on Tim. He began thinking of the tremendous number of people held in captivity. The gas chambers, ovens, and mass graves began to make an impact on Tim when he read the tremendous number of people killed at this one location. The one number, which stuck in Tim's mind, was the thirty-two thousand people liberated on April 29, 1945, by the US military troops. Tim made up his mind that his report was going to focus on the liberation of the Holocaust survivors.

When the entire club met back at their hotel for the second night in Munich, some kind of a protest was being conducted in the street in front of their hotel. Mrs. Schmidt tried to corral her students and told the chaperones to keep everyone walking.

Mrs. Schmidt said, "I want everyone to keep walking. Don't say anything. Don't interact with anyone."

The club students saw a number of protesters with signs calling for the fall of the United States. The signs called the United States imperialist. Tim and Brett saw some protesters burning an American flag. When the students entered the safety of their hotel, Mrs. Schmidt said, "I would like everyone to come to my room. It will be a tight fit, but I want to talk to everyone." She then led the way to room number 108.

When everyone was gathered in her room, Mrs. Schmidt said, "Many of you may have never seen a protest up close. I believe these protesters were specifically targeting us as Americans. I don't believe they will harm us as long as we don't confront them or argue with them. If we should respond, something could get out of control very quickly."

One student asked, "Mrs. Schmidt, I know the protesters back home were burning draft cards. Why are the Germans calling us imperialists? We are trying to help the people in Vietnam. We're not trying to occupy their country."

Mrs. Schmidt, said, "Some countries are concerned with the US escalating the war at times when the North Vietnamese give indications they wanted peace. Some also feel like the war is immoral and interferes with the self-determination of the Vietnamese people."

A student said, "Mrs. Schmidt, my brother is in the military. I came close to yelling something at the protesters burning our flag."

Mrs. Schmidt replied, "So did I. However, your safety is my primary concern. If any protesters confront us again, I must insist that you all stay together and don't reply. They are trained to stir up trouble, and they are hoping you will say or do something. I support your right to protest against other protesters. However, we all need to support one another in a time of potential trouble. I can't let my rights or your rights put us all in danger."

The remainder of the trip did not involve any protesters. In fact, the German people overwhelmingly welcomed the students. The students enjoyed the historical places and beautiful sights.

Mrs. Schmidt spoke to everyone on the bus as they were heading toward Schwaebisch Hall. She said, "Some of you have asked me what to look for at our last stop. I have always tried to avoid answering that question. First, I respectfully ask that you do not tell future clubs what to expect at this stop. I like to keep this last stop as a surprise. Schwaebisch Hall is my hometown. The town is a quaint, quiet little farming village. As we approach the town, you will begin to notice farms but no barns or homes. The farms surround the town, but the farmers all live in the town. When we arrive, I would like for everyone to walk around town leading up to our dinner. I want you to see and experience a typical German hometown. I have a number of my family joining us for dinner. The town Burgermeister, or Mayor, will join us for dinner. In addition, the commander of a nearby United States military base will join us as well. They typically give a little speech and then take questions. For those of you who think they should sneak a beer on the last night of the trip, I must remind you that you all signed an agreement to not drink any beer. I bring this to your attention because the owner of the guesthouse has a strong opinion that beer is better for you than any soda. Actually, she is correct. She has also been known to discreetly serve beer in a soda bottle."

Everyone laughed.

It didn't take long for the students to discover that the owner of the guesthouse was, in fact, Mrs. Schmidt's mother.

One student said, "I am going to do my report on the benefits of beer."

CHAPTER 17

Tim and Brett continued to enjoy vacations together at Cooper's Camp every summer. They were also classmates throughout high school. Upon graduation from high school, the two friends were happy to attend college together. Unfortunately, the war in Vietnam was escalating. The ranks of the military were being supplemented by the government's use of the draft. Initially, Tim and Brett appeared to be exempt from the draft, in that, as freshman college students, they had received a student deferment from the draft. However, on October 31, 1967, Timothy Sands received a notice from the selective service. The notice advised Tim that his student deferment of a 4S had been withdrawn and his new status was upgraded to 1A.

Tim and Brett had a long discussion. They knew that a draft notice of 1A was a fancy way of saying, "You are soon going to war." It was also common knowledge that draftees were typically assigned to the infantry. It was also known that the life expectancy of an infantryman was generally tabulated in a time frame of weeks, not months. Tim needed to know what his options would be if he enlisted. Tim would need to visit the US Army recruiter. Brett wanted to tag along.

Staff Sergeant Pearson introduced himself as the local recruiter for the United States Army. He said, "If you have what it takes, I'm willing to walk you through the induction process and have you both in uniform within two weeks."

Tim said, "First, I'm really not anxious to be in uniform within two weeks. In addition, Brett is just here as my friend. He still has a student deferment. I'm the one with the 1A status."

Staff Sergeant Pearson said, "Okay, no problem. If you don't want to be in uniform and your friend is exempt from the draft, exactly how can I help?"

Tim said, "I really don't know. I just want to know what I can expect if I get drafted."

Staff Sergeant Pearson said, "So you are concerned about being drafted. That I understand. We have no control over the draft. However, your 1A status means you will soon be in uniform. It's just a matter of time."

Tim said, "It's common knowledge that draftees are generally assigned to the infantry. Is that true?"

Staff Sergeant Pearson said, "That's generally true. Draftees are typically infantrymen, and they serve two years of active duty. I can offer you the possibility of a better MOS if you enlist for three years of active duty."

Tim asked, "What is an MOS?"

The staff sergeant said, "Sorry, we use a lot of acronyms. MOS means 'Military Occupational Battery.' It's a brief way to describe your training. So we give you a series of tests. Depending on how well you do, we have a list of jobs for which you could apply. Since you are in college, you might do really well on the tests. If you do well on the tests, we give you another series of tests. This could open even more opportunities. I can't tell you what jobs would be available until you take the ASVAB. That's the Armed Services Vocational Aptitude Battery."

Tim said, "Just for clarification, I take a test which determines what jobs are available. If I enlist for three years, I get to choose a job on that list. Correct?"

Staff Sergeant Pearson said, "That is correct. I can guarantee your training will be in the job you select from the list produced based upon your ASVAB scores."

Tim said, "And if I wait until I get drafted, do I still take the ASVAB?"

Staff Sergeant Pearson said, "Yes. We still want to know if you have a brain. But you will not have any choice in your job training. The Army will use a draftee to fill the most needed positions. We generally need more infantrymen."

Tim said, "And generally you need more infantrymen because…"

Staff Sergeant Pearson said, "Yes, the war has taken a heavy toll on the infantry."

Tim said, "Okay, I will take the test."

Brett said, "Me too."

Tim said, "Brett, you don't need this. You're still safe."

Brett said, "I just want to see if I can get a better score than you."

That night, Tim had a long conversation with his parents. Brett did so as well.

*****

Two weeks later, Tim and Brett were each looking at a list of military job opportunities provided by Staff Sergeant Pearson.

Tim and Brett looked carefully at a very long list of job opportunities. They had both scored extremely well.

Tim said, "Brett, every time I go through this list, I keep coming back to the job of a medic."

Brett said, "I thought about that as well."

Tim said, "Brett, this is not about you. You can't do this. I am the one that needs to do this."

Brett said, "Tim, two weeks ago, I said I wanted to take the test just to be competitive. However, two days ago, I got my 1A notice. It now appears we are both in the same boat."

Tim and Brett gave each other a high five.

Tim said, "Sergeant Pearson, tell us what you can about serving as a medic."

Staff Sergeant Pearson said, "A medic is probably among the top ten hardest jobs in the military. It will not be easy. However, when the crap hits the fan, the first call always goes out for a medic."

Brett said, "What is the life expectancy for a medic?"

Staff Sergeant Pearson said, "Any amount of time in combat has an impact upon your life expectancy. However, one element of the Geneva Convention declares medical personnel cannot intentionally be killed. To do so could result in being charged with a war crime. However, I don't think a dead person can object to the actions by others as being intentional or unintentional."

Tim said, "If we both enlist, what will be the odds that we will go to Vietnam?"

Staff Sergeant Pearson said, "It's actually best to plan on going to Vietnam. Then if you don't go, you can brag about how lucky you are."

Brett said, "Sergeant Pearson, with all due respect, right now I don't feel like luck is on my side."

Staff Sergeant Pearson said, "If you both sign up, I can process your induction under the buddy system. This would guarantee you're staying with your buddy through basic training and throughout your advanced individual training. After training, all bets are off. Your first duty assignments will probably not be the same."

CHAPTER 18

On December 27, 1967, Timothy Sands and Brett Corson were standing in a group of inductees and told to raise their right hand and repeat the following:

"I (state your name) do solemnly swear that I will support and defend the Constitution of the United States against all enemies, foreign and domestic; that I will bear true faith and allegiance to the same; and that I will obey the orders of the president of the United States and the orders of the officers appointed over me, according to regulations and the Uniform Code of Military Justice. So help me, God."

The remainder of the day consisted of standing in line for haircuts; standing in line for uniforms, boots, sheets, blankets, and personal gear; and standing in line for meals. In fact, standing in line was a newly learned activity, whereas your eyes were focused on the back of the head of the person in front of you and your chest was pressed against the back of the person in front of you. Even eating in the mess hall was a newly learned activity. Each person ate what was served, there was no need for talking, and the drill sergeants determined the allotted time for food consumption. Generally, the allotted time was so short that everyone learned to eat very quickly.

Basic training was a whirlwind of seemingly chaotic confusion. Yet as time progressed, the yelling and running and marching all began to produce teamwork, strength development, endurance, and skillful marksmanship. Classes focused on learning the Army values. These values included loyalty, duty, respect, selfless service, honor, integrity, and personal courage.

The drills, running, marching, obstacle courses, and inspections became routine. Repetition leads to memory. When recruits repeat the assembly and disassembly of a weapon, this learning helps translate a skill from a conscious act to a subconscious memory. Thus, repetition helps to create long-term memory.

Teamwork and dependency upon each other, as a team, are critical to the building of cohesion, confidence, and trust in leadership. The basic training experience gave recruits an ability to make it through obstacles together. They also learned that the team would never quit. Failure is not an option.

Private Timothy Sands and Private Brett Corson were excited about having their respective families attend the graduation ceremonies from the US Army, ten-week basic training at Fort Dix, New Jersey. The graduates demonstrated their marching skills, marksmanship skills, and recognition of personal awards. Private Timothy Sands was awarded the company "leadership" award. Private Brett Corson was awarded the "honor" award, based upon one of the seven Army values.

Immediately following the basic training graduation, Tim and Brett were granted a weekend leave. They were able to go home with their parents. The two days off seemed to be a flash in time. The two friends spent quality time and a home-cooked meal with family. However, their travel orders were cut for air travel from the Philadelphia International Airport to Houston, Texas, for Monday, April 2, 1968.

CHAPTER 19

Timothy Sands, private second class (E-2), and Brett Corson, private second class (E-2), reported for duty at Fort Sam Houston, home of the combat medic training facility. The privates were embarking on their advanced training as combat medics, with an MOS of a 91A. They would soon find that lectures, field training, and study would be challenging. The training they would receive would be a high level of emergency medical training. They would be taught complicated skills along with the ability to think. They would need to make quick lifesaving decisions to include when to do something and when not to do something.

The first week of advanced individual training began with seven days of kitchen patrol (KP). The success of a military unit is dependent upon a well-fed corps. The mess hall requires the dedicated efforts of cooks to plan, prepare, and serve three well-balanced meals a day. Soldiers assigned to KP were responsible for washing pots, pans, trays, silverware, floors, tables, and anything related to the cleanliness of the mess hall. The hours were long, and the work was generally disliked. However, the training of soldiers in a systematic manner would be better served if the students in training did not miss any class time to pull KP duty. Therefore, the training began with seven days of KP duty, and then the students would not be required to miss any class time for the remainder of their course of study.

Tim and Brett were fully engaged in the process of learning the basics of emergency medical treatment of critically wounded soldiers. The training included typical cardiopulmonary resuscitation (CPR), application of emergency medical skills, fluid resuscitation, administration of medication, treatment of wounds, and effective use of tourniquets. These areas of study and others were presented in classrooms, put into practice on the classroom floors using classmates as patients, and translated into tests to determine if the students would eventually qualify as combat medics.

The latter portion of the training included the weapons qualification for the use of a colt .45 pistol. This was the weapon issued to combat medics and intended for use in personal protection.

The students in medic training were also introduced to the helicopter as the primary means of evacuation in jungle warfare. The medics in training would learn how to coordinate the proper loading and unloading of patients in an evacuation helicopter.

Timothy Sands graduated from his advanced individual training with the highest score among his class. Tim was awarded the MOS 91A as a combat medic and received a promotion to private first class (E-3).

Brett Corson graduated with the highest score on the range. Brett received an expert weapons badge for the pistol. Brett was also awarded the MOS 91A and received a promotion to private first class (E-3).

Tim and Brett both received orders for a thirty-day leave. However, their orders also included a reporting date of September 1, 1968, to Fort Dix, New Jersey, for a future assignment under the command of General William C. Westmoreland, commander, US Military Assistance Command, Vietnam (MACV), a joint-service command of the United States Department of Defense.

Part 3

The Adventures
of a Soldier

The LORD is my strength and my shield; my
heart trusts in Him, and He helps me.

—Psalm 28:7 (KJV)

CHAPTER 20

Tim and Brett reported to Fort Dix, New Jersey, on September 1, 1968, as ordered. The friends were assigned to a holding unit while they waited for their names to appear on a transport list. Each day, one or two lists of names would be posted on a bulletin board. The list would identify the individuals and departure time for those being shipped out. Those in waiting for Vietnam were only allowed to bring a small amount of personal items. They would be issued combat duty clothing upon arrival in Vietnam. If the two friends did not ship out on the same flight, in all likelihood, they would be separated in their future assignments.

Private Timothy Sands's name appeared on the 8:00 a.m. departure for September 5, 1968. Private Brett Corson's name appeared on the 11:00 a.m. departure for September 5, 1968. The buddy system had held up throughout training. Now the two best friends were going on separate war adventures.

Private Timothy Sands said goodbye to Brett and climbed aboard one of several buses taking him and 250 other soldiers to the nearby airfield at the McGuire Air Force Base. Timothy took his window seat on the military transport airplane and buckled his seat belt for a flight that would take him halfway around the world. The atmosphere during this flight was subdued. The passengers had taken an oath to defend against all enemies. They all completed the necessary basic military training. They had all completed their advanced individual training. Now they were heading to a country they had heard about and an enemy they were trained to kill. The reality of war was beginning to settle in. There was not much to talk about on this twenty-four-hour journey.

The military aircraft landed at McCord Air Force Base, Washington. The passengers disembarked and walked across the tarmac and boarded a chartered Flying Tiger, DC 8, stripped down version of an all-coach-class commercial airplane. The seating on this airplane was less comfortable than the military aircraft. The Flying Tiger departed for Saigon, Vietnam, with stops at Anchorage, Alaska, and Yokota Air Base in Japan.

Tim had a window seat on the Flying Tiger airplane. As the airplane began its descent in preparation for landing, Tim had an opportunity to observe the country he would see, smell, and taste over the next twelve months. Tim could see nothing but dense forest, pockets of smoke, and very few roads. Surprisingly, the airport in Saigon was much larger than Tim had anticipated.

Tim realized that the Flying Tiger airplane he and his fellow passengers had departed was immediately boarded by soldiers leaving, having served their time in this war. The Flying Tiger was quickly loaded and taxiing for takeoff. Obviously, the airplane crew was anxious to get off the ground as soon as possible.

Tim and his fellow passengers were loaded onto buses en route to the Long Binh Post. The newbies would be delivered to the Army Ninetieth Replacement Battalion. This would be a temporary holding place while waiting for a permanent unit assignment. In addition, the newbies would receive their initial issue of jungle uniforms, boots, hats, and essentials. The unit of assignment would distribute the final issue of combat weaponry.

Tim was in the Ninetieth Replacement Battalion for three days. On the third day, his name appeared on the assignment sheet. Private Timothy Sands was assigned to the 25th Infantry Division, 159th Medical Detachment, Chu Chi. His flight to Chu Chi airfield would be 0900 hours, September 10, 1968. This date would be the first day of his countdown. Private Timothy Sands would be assigned to the 159th Medical Detachment for the next 365 days.

Tim and his fellow soldiers boarded a C-123 aircraft for a twenty-minute flight to Chu Chi. The arrival at the Chu Chi airfield gave Tim a new awareness of his senses. The temperature was extremely hot. Vehicles were practically consumed with their own dust. Artillery guns were extremely loud. The smell of sulfur, dust, smoke, and something else was hard to ignore. What was that smell? Tim would soon find out the stinky smell was the product of barrels of human waste mixed with kerosene or diesel fuel and burned.

CHAPTER 21

Private Timothy Sands reported to the 159th Medical Detachment. His permanent assignment would include the issuance of his final complement of necessities. Private Sands was issued his flak jacket, steel pot helmet with its liner, gas mask, M-16 rifle and M9 pistol, with ammunition, ammunition belt, and cleaning kits for the weapons. He was issued a sheet, blanket, rain gear, and a pillow. As a combat medic, Private Sands was issued an empty medic's bag.

The supply sergeant anticipated a question with regards to an empty medic's bag and said, "Private Sands, you will be given your medical supplies from your medical team at the hospital. This is all the stuff I can give you. Besides, it's all the stuff you can carry at the moment."

Tim said, "Thank you, Sergeant."

Tim was about to ask where to go from here, and someone said, "Timothy Sands, you are with me. My name is Jack Jackson. Let me give you a hand carrying some of that stuff."

Tim recognized that Jack Jackson was a corporal. Jack Jackson reached for the blankets and pillow and stuff. He was not offering to carry Tim's weapons. Tim was glad because he wasn't sure how to say no to someone with a higher rank.

Jack Jackson said, "We are in the same hooch. You are assigned to my unit. Once I get you settled in, I need to take you to our division commander and then to our unit commander."

Tim said, "Corporal Jackson—"

Jack interrupted. "Unless we are around the brass, just call me Jack. Did you have a question?"

Tim said, "Yeah, what is that awful smell?"

Jack said, "Lunch."

They both laughed.

Jack led Tim down a wooden boardwalk. The walkway was a network of parallel telephone poles lying on the ground about six feet apart. Boards were nailed to connect the poles, thus creating a boardwalk. It was pretty obvious that the raised boardwalks would be helpful during the monsoon rains.

Jack stopped in front of a wooden building and said, "Here is home."

Home was affectingly referred to as the "hooch." The hooch was a wooden structure, wooden floor, and screened-in walls with a metal roof, which extended well past the walls. This roof overhang was helpful to shed heavy rains from completely washing out the hooch. The outside walls were protected with sandbags, which were stacked about four feet high. A hooch was home to eight or ten soldiers.

Each group of six hooches shared a common bunker. The bunker was an aboveground shelter made of sandbags with a metal roof and covered with sandbags. These shelters were used during mortar and rocket attacks.

Jack said, "Tim, you and I are neighbors. Your bunk area is directly across from me. Let's just set your stuff down on your bunk for now. Put your weapons in the locker. You need to report to our commanding officer and unit commander as soon as possible."

Jack led Tim to the 25th Infantry, 159th Medical Detachment headquarters. Colonel Ron Buck was the detachment divisional commander.

Private Timothy Sands stood at attention with a salute. "Sir, Private Timothy Sands reporting for duty, sir."

Colonel Buck returned the salute without moving from his chair.

"Stand at ease, Private Sands."

Colonel Buck opened a folder and said, "Private Sands, I see you are from New Jersey."

"Yes, sir."

"I also see that you graduated first in your class at Fort Sam Houston."

"Yes, sir."

"Private Sands, you will be working with our helicopter medevac unit. The mission of this unit is simply saving lives. Your training and skills will be tested, but more importantly, your devotion to duty and character will be confirmed. I will do all that I can to support you in fulfilling your assigned work. Private Sands, are you ready to work along with me to make this unit successful?"

"Yes, sir, I am."

Colonel Buck stood up and shook private Sand's hand and said, "Welcome to the Twenty-Fifth."

Private Timothy Sands snapped to attention and offered a sharp salute.

Colonel Buck returned the salute and said, "Welcome aboard, Sands. You are dismissed."

Private Timothy Sands did an about-face and departed Colonel Buck's office. Tim had never even met someone of the rank of a colonel, yet he felt comfortable with Colonel Buck and appreciated his support.

Jack took Tim to the unit commander.

The 159th Medical Detachment was under the command of Major James Young. Tim was welcomed by Major Young and assigned to work with Corporal Jack Jackson. Tim felt that his commanders were truly dedicated to the fulfillment of their mission.

Jack said, "Tim, let's get your medical supplies. I will walk you around the hospital and then lunch. After we eat, I will take you over to the airport. Tomorrow, you go to work."

Tim said, "I'm okay with everything except lunch."

Jack introduced Tim to several doctors, nurses, medics, pilots, and helicopter crew members. Tim was impressed with the medical professionalism demonstrated in the transport and care of the wounded soldiers. One stop, which Jack had not announced, was a visit to the morgue.

Tim said, "Why the visit to the morgue?"

"Just for a reality check. We are not always successful in saving lives. We do our best, but life and death are controlled by God, not us."

Jack and Tim sat down for lunch. Tim said, "Actually, the food isn't too bad."

Jack said, "Don't worry. It will get worse."

Jack asked, "So what do you think of our unit?"

Tim said, "I'm glad to have you as my mentor. You are well liked by the medical and air professionals. That means a lot to me."

Jack said, "Well, we have a good team. In addition, this is a good assignment. You could have been assigned to an infantry unit. That can be a hard assignment. Don't get me wrong. We will have some bad days. But at the end of the day, we have access to a cold shower, a squeaky cot with a pillow, and a cooked meal. You have a lot for which to be thankful."

Tim said, "I am"

Jack said, "Let's get your medical gear packed for tomorrow. We bring our weapons and medic bags on every mission. We work twelve hours on and twelve hours off for three hundred and sixty-five. For you, that's three hundred and sixty-four. For me, that is exactly a hundred and forty-eight."

Tim said, "Will that be around the end of January?"

Jack said, "It will be on February 5, 1969. That will also be around when you make corporal and take over for me."

For Private Timothy Sands, day one in the Twenty-Fifth Medical Detachment was a very busy day. He was tired, and even the poor condition of the cot would not hinder his sleep. However, the constant firing of artillery will make it difficult to sleep.

CHAPTER 22

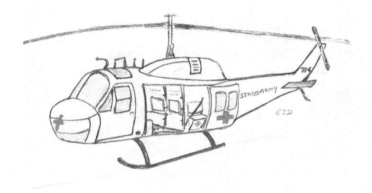

Corporal Jack Jackson introduced Private Timothy Sands to the pilot and crew of air ambulance 786. The Bell UH-1 Huey helicopter with a tail number of 786 was a dedicated medical air ambulance. This designation allowed for the helicopter to display a medical red cross and the pilot's use of a "dust off" as a call sign. *Dust off* is the acronym for "*d*edicated *u*nhesitating *s*ervice *t*o *o*ur *f*ighting *f*orces. The pilots and crew of a medical helicopter received advanced medical training. The aircraft was modified to officially accommodate the transport of six-litter causalities. It was known that there were occasions when eight to twelve casualties were transported at one time.

The crew of dust off 786 reported to their helicopter at 0600 hours for a preflight checklist. In the event of a call for a medical evacuation, the Huey would be airborne within three minutes. When the crew was assured the helicopter was ready, they sat down in the dispatch center for a cup of coffee. Lieutenant Richard Kolish was the pilot for this aircraft today. Lieutenant Dennis Cordrey was a pilot.

However, for this assignment, he would be the commander. As the commander, he would navigate, monitor all the radio communications, and identify and communicate with the ground unit requesting the medevac. Naturally, if the pilot was injured, the commander would fly the aircraft. Sergeant Mike Furst was the crew chief. He maintained the helicopter and kept things running smoothly.

Lieutenant Cordrey said, "Private Sands, since this is your first day on the job, I have a couple of things that need to be understood. First, you do whatever Corporal Jackson tells you to do, and you do it without hesitation. Understood?"

Tim Sands replied, "Yes, sir, I understand."

Lieutenant Cordrey said, "The second thing you need to understand is that I am the commander and you are the medic. I will tell you what to do for the safety of this crew. You will do what you are trained to do to care for the wounded. I am the commander, and you are the doctor. You listen to me, and I will listen to you. We are a team. When we are on a mission, our radio communication will be brief and direct. Clear communication is necessary. Poor communication is dangerous. Understood?"

Tim Sands replied, "Yes, sir, I understand."

Lieutenant Cordrey said, "Okay, crew, since we have a new doctor on board, let's go on a training mission to teach this newbie a few things."

Lieutenant Richard Kolish fired up the helicopter, and within a few minutes, the crew confirmed that each one was connected through their helmet headphones and microphone. Lieutenant Kolish said, "Chu Chi tower, dust off 786, for departure. Nonemergency."

"Dust off 786, zero wind, altimeter 39.92, using runway 09."

"Chu Chi, dust off 786 understands, zero wind, altimeter 39.92, runway 09, requesting takeoff."

"Dust off 786, taxi to runway 09. Hold for the C-123 on final approach."

"Chu Chi, dust off 786 understands taxi to runway 09 and hold."

Lieutenant Kolish flew the helicopter above the taxiway to the edge of runway 09 and held it in a hover position.

"Dust off 786, you are clear for takeoff, runway 09."

"Chu Chi, dust off 786 roger takeoff. Thank you."

"Dust off 786, contact flight following, have a great flight."

Private Timothy Sands was airborne on his first training flight as a combat medic. Within fifteen minutes, the training flight turned into a medevac. Tim would now put his training into action. He listened carefully for the details of the nine-line. The slogan "Low-flying pilots eat tacos" helps to identify the first five of the nine-line.

Line one: *Low* is the *L*, for location or pickup site for the medevac.

Line two: *Flying* is the *F*, for the radio frequency used by the flight commander and the combat unit in the field.

Line three: *Pilots* is the *P*, for number of patients by priority.

Line four: *Eat* is the *E*, for special equipment required for this mission.

Line five: *Tacos* is the *T*, for type of patients, such as litter or ambulatory.

Lines six, seven, eight, and nine were identified only as needed.

Line six: Security for the pickup site was communicated to the flight commander as an alert to the presence of enemy troops in the area or if an armed escort was necessary.

Line seven: Security for identifying the pickup location was communicated to the flight commander. Typically, the ground unit would pop a smoke canister, and the flight commander would identify and confirm the color of the smoke.

Line eight: If necessary, the patient's nationality and status would be shared with the flight commander. The information may specify the patient's status as US military, US civilian, non-US military, non-US civilian, or any of the above as "killed in action" (KIA).

The least-used line was number nine. This identified any NBC contamination: *N* for "nuclear," *B* for "biological," and *C* for "chemical."

It was important for the medic to know the number of patients and their status. Tim confirmed with Jack that this medevac would expect two urgent litter patients and two ambulatory.

Flight Commander Cordrey had several communications with the ground unit and the pilot. Finally, he said, "Crew, we are going in with possible enemy on the starboard side. Two critical litters and two ambulatory."

Pilot Kolish replied, "Roger."

Crew Chief Furst replied, "Roger."

Medic Jackson replied, "Roger."

Medic Sands replied, "Roger."

Corporal Jackson said, "Sands, we will load from the port side."

As the helicopter touched down, the medics jumped to the ground and assisted with lifting the litters into the helicopter. The crew chief remained on the helicopter and assisted with the loading of the litters and the two ambulatory cases. Within three minutes, the patients were loaded, and the crew chief said, "Commander, we are loaded and clear on the starboard."

Medic Jackson said, "Commander, we are secure and clear on the port."

Commander Cordrey said, "Clear for takeoff. Possible incoming starboard side."

Pilot Kolish said, "Taking off port side."

When the helicopter was clear of the pickup site, Commander Cordrey said, "Doc, give me a status report on our guests."

Medic Jackson said, "Commander, two litters serious but stable with clear airways, one with leg injury, one leg and arm injuries. The two ambulatory have routine injuries. Our guests will be comfortable."

Commander Cordrey said, "Roger. I will alert the hospital staff."

After this medevac mission, the crew of dust off 786 had an unusually quiet afternoon. They were in the dispatch center with two other ambulatory crews. A few individuals had engaged in a game of poker.

Lieutenant Dennis Cordrey sat at a table across from Private Timothy Sands and said, "Well, Doc, you did well on your first dust off."

Private Sands replied, "Thank you, sir. I was a little nervous at first."

Lieutenant Cordrey said, "Everyone is nervous on their first mission. I was watching your medical treatment of the wounded.

You did what was necessary, and you didn't need to be told what to do by Corporal Jackson. Since today has been a little slow, I will give you one more day as a ride-along with Corporal Jackson. After that, you will be on your own."

Private Sands replied, "Yes, sir. If you think I am ready to go solo."

Lieutenant Cordrey said, "I think you will be fine. I just need to make sure we don't continue to carry two medics when we may need that space on the helicopter for another wounded."

Private Sands said, "Thank you for sharing your concern. I understand, and I appreciate your confidence in me."

CHAPTER 23

Private Timothy Sands joined with Corporal Jack Jackson on their second day of duty together on dust off 786. The crew of dust off 786 was the same, and Tim understood this would be his final day with Jack. Lieutenant Dennis Cordrey made it clear he didn't need two medics flying together. The crew of dust off 786 was alerted that several troops were reporting enemy engagements. This may prove to be a busy day.

The first four missions of the day gave Tim exposure to the treatment of critically injured soldiers. Jack was pleased with Tim's ability to treat some problematic chest injuries and airway complications. However, as the sun was setting, a priority medevac mission was called out. Dust off 786 would take the mission. Nighttime missions presented several concerns for safety. If the helicopter pilot turned on its landing lights, this would present the aircraft as an easy target. If the ground unit used lights to assist the helicopter pilot, they presented themselves as an easy target. This particular mission was just around dusk. The setting sun was providing just enough light to land without the use of lights, but time was running short. The mission was necessary because the ground unit had declared it a high priority.

Commander Cordrey was communicating with the ground unit to determine the nine-line details of this medevac. This particular mission was going to be challenging. The ground unit was under enemy fire, so the landing zone (LZ) would be hot. They did not have time to wait for a gunship escort. Most disturbing for Tim was the news that one of the critically wounded soldiers was the ground unit's only medic. Tim immediately thought about the unit, under fire, without a medic.

Tim spoke into his microphone. "Commander, I need to replace this ground unit's medic."

The response was, "What did you say?"

Tim said, "Commander, the ground unit needs a medic."

Commander Cordrey replied, "I don't like the idea."

Tim said, "Commander, with all due respect, you have two medics. They don't have any."

Commander Cordrey said, "Private Sands, you better not make me regret this decision."

Within the time frame of five minutes, Tim was kneeling on the ground, holding his medic's bag while watching dust off 786 flying off into the sunset. With the sound of the helicopter fading, Tim heard gunshots and someone yelling, "*Medic.*"

Private Timothy Sands worked throughout the night.

At first light, Lieutenant Willis Fox sat down with Private Sands and said, "Welcome to the Third Brigade, Fourth Infantry." Lieutenant Fox then offered Tim a meal and said, "Sorry I can't offer you anything better. It's all we have."

Private Timothy Sands took the individual C-ration meal, which was marked "spaghetti with meatballs." Tim proceeded to open the meal. He was going to eat whatever was offered. When Tim came upon the small pack of cigarettes, he offered them to Lieutenant Willis. He said, "Do you want these? I don't smoke."

Lieutenant Willis Fox said, "Private Sands, cigarettes are the most valuable item in a C-ration meal. You don't just give them away. Your uniform looks awfully new. Tell me. Private, how long have you been in-country?"

Private Timothy Sands replied, "Sir, six days."

Lieutenant Fox said, "Well, Private Sands, for a newbie, you did one heck of a job last night. From what I understand from your flight commander, you volunteered to help us out. Is that correct?"

Private Sands said, "Yes, sir, I was on the dust off for training. However, when I heard that your medic was critically wounded, I couldn't just leave your unit without any medical assistance. It didn't make sense that two medics would fly away and leave you with no one."

Lieutenant Fox offered his hand and said, "Thank you."

The two shook hands.

After a few minutes of silence, Lieutenant Fox said, "I'm not a big religious guy, but you are an answer to prayer. When our medic went down, I knew we would not get a replacement until daybreak. I prayed a 'foxhole prayer' for God to do something to help us, in exchange for a promise from me. A few minutes later, your flight commander said he was *loaning* us a first-rate medic. He seemed to emphasize the word *loaning*. I guess that means we can't keep you. Unless, in fact, I appeal to the divisional commander that you volunteered."

Tim said, "Sir, you're talking way above my pay grade."

Lieutenant Fox stood up and said aloud, "All those in favor of keeping this medic as our own doctor, say *yeah*."

There was a loud *yeah*.

Lieutenant Fox sat down and said, "Private Sands, I'm just playing around with you. Our unit is sending us a new medic. Maybe today. I'm trying to get some supplies shipped in and at the same time a transport-out, for our fallen. We lost two men yesterday. I can only hope that you would consider it an honor to fly out with our fallen. You stood by us, and I appreciate what you did."

Tim said, "Sir, can I ask a question?"

"Ask."

Tim asked, "Why didn't you ship the fallen soldiers out on the dust off?"

Lieutenant Fox said, "That's a good question. Sometimes, the dust off flight commanders will allow for the transport for those killed in action (KIA) if the process doesn't endanger the life of the wounded. We had some pretty bad injuries yesterday. I couldn't jeopardize a time delay for the sake of our injured and for the safety of the dust off, as the sun was going down. Minutes matter to the living. I am expecting a supply shipment today, and they will transport our fallen. If I weren't scheduled for a supply shipment, I would call out for a casevac. A casevac is a callout for help from any helicopter in the area, which may be available to transport our fallen."

Tim said, "Could a dust off respond to a casevac? When I was on my first training flight, we were available."

Lieutenant Fox said, "Your flight commander may not like the idea of using his air ambulance as a hearse."

Tim responded, "I understand. Lieutenant Fox, when your supplies arrive, I will consider it an honor to escort your fallen soldiers back to our base camp."

The enemy had retreated, and Tim was told his replacement was scheduled to arrive by noon. Tim removed a notebook from his medic's bag and wrote down the names of the two fallen soldiers he would soon escort back to the base camp. Tim sat under a tree within sight of the fallen soldiers and wondered if he would ever get a chance to meet their families.

Tim flew back to base camp. As his transport helicopter was landing, the flight commander said, "Private Sands, I just received a message for you to report to Colonel Buck's office immediately. I sure hope you didn't screw up."

Tim replied, "Sir, I hope not."

Tim reported to Colonel Buck's office and found Lieutenant Dennis Cordrey waiting for him in an outer office.

Tim said, "Lieutenant Cordrey, I sure hope this thing didn't get you in trouble. I take full responsibility."

Lieutenant Cordrey replied, "Private Sands, I stand by my decision. Let's face the music together."

Lieutenant Cordrey and Private Sands reported to Colonel Ron Buck.

Colonel Buck said, "Stand at ease, gentlemen."

Colonel Buck took a draw from his cigar. He then said, "I found out from Major Doug Schow from the Third Brigade that Private Timothy Sands spent last night with his Fourth Infantry Unit. I am not sure how this could happen since Private Sands is currently under the supervision of my lieutenant, Dennis Cordrey. Perhaps my lieutenant would explain why he thought it was such a good idea to let a private, with less than a week in country, spend the night with a ground unit, which was under intense enemy fire?"

Lieutenant Cordrey said, "Colonel, I believe the critical issue at hand was the fact that the infantry unit's medic was critically wounded. At the moment of our medevac, I had two medics on board dust off 786. Private Timothy Sands brought to my attention that a decision to fly away with two medics while the ground unit had none would be an irresponsible decision."

Colonel Buck said, "Lieutenant, you didn't answer my question. Why did you think it was a good idea to let a private, with less than a week in country, spend the night with a ground unit under intense enemy fire? Didn't you have a corporal on board dust off 786? If you felt it necessary to leave one of your medics in a combat situation, why didn't you leave the corporal?"

Lieutenant Cordrey said, "Colonel Buck, with all due respect, in the brief time I had observed the medical skills of private Timothy Sands, I felt he had the skills and courage to carry out this assignment. I stand by my decision that a medic was needed and Private Sands was the man for the mission."

Colonel Buck said, "Private Sands, I understand you volunteered for this mission. What do you have to say for yourself?"

Private Timothy Sands said, "Sir, on my first day in country, you were kind enough to welcome me. You said our mission is to save lives. That's why I volunteered to replace a critically wounded medic and hopefully save lives."

Colonel Buck took another long draw on his cigar.

"I don't like it when a ground unit tries to steal one of my men. The reason Major Doug Schow called is his lieutenant, Willis Fox, from the Fourth Infantry wanted to request a personnel transfer. He wanted me to approve and transfer private Timothy Sands to his unit. Tell me, Lieutenant Cordrey, do you think it is a good idea to let Private Sands transfer to the Third Brigade?"

Lieutenant Cordrey said, "Sir, I oppose any effort by any unit to steal private Timothy Sands."

Colonel Buck said, "Tell me, Private Sands, did you volunteer to serve with the Third Brigade as a means of leaving this unit?"

Private Sands replied, "Sir, no, sir."

Colonel Buck said, "Gentlemen, I commend you both. When Major Doug Schow realized I was not going to approve his request, he advised me that his lieutenant, Willis Fox, is planning to recommend an Army Commendation Medal for each of you. Any questions?"

Neither man spoke up.

Colonel Buck said, "Good job. Thank you."

That night, after a long cold shower, Tim sat on the edge of his bed and wrote in his journal.

> Sunday, September 15, 1968—Countdown—359 days
>
> Last night, I was with the Fourth Infantry Unit someplace in the jungle. Their medic was seriously injured, and I took his place. I was definitely afraid, but I treated their wounded.
>
> I flew back to the base camp with Corporal Dale Kile and Private Robert Woods. I talked to them. I told them I would do my best to visit their resting place and their families when I get back to the States.
>
> I have a new appreciation for a roof over my head and cot with a pillow.
>
> Thank you, Lord.
>
> I am tired. Good night.
> Overcomer

CHAPTER 24

Tim found out just how beneficial the roof over his head and the raised wooden sidewalks were due to a week of monsoon rains. During the monsoon season, the mud and flooded areas around the base camp made it difficult to get around. On the good side of things, the combat fighting generally stopped, and Tim's dust off team was grounded. In situations like this, several medics would spend time in the Twelfth Evacuation Hospital and provide some relief to the nursing staff in caring for patients.

The Twelfth Evacuation Hospital was a permanent surgical complex, which had replaced the former Seventh Mobile Army Surgical Hospital (MASH) Unit. The utilization of a MASH Unit was an attempt to move surgical units closer to the wounded. With the advancements in air medevacs, it became an enhancement in surgical care to establish a permanent medical complex.

The Twelfth Evacuation Hospital was able to successfully handle a large number of wounded. The surgical complex had two long rows of Quonset-type buildings with maybe thirty to forty yards between the two rows. The first row of buildings contained an emergency triage area. The adjacent buildings contained radiology, pre-operative care, and then operating buildings. The post-operative buildings progressed from post-operative and intensive care units and, finally, several medical units. All of the buildings were connected with the typical raised wood sidewalks. The triage area was adjacent to the two helicopter landing pads. During the height of combat activity, this hospital would process as many as thirty or fifty wounded with additional dust off helicopters waiting in line for drop-offs.

Private Timothy Sands was happy to work with the medical staff in providing care for those in post-operative care or in the medical care units. Occasionally, Tim was able to connect with one of the patients he had cared for during a medevac.

On one particular visit at the Twelfth Surgical Hospital, Private Timothy Sands had an opportunity to shadow Captain Lloyd Moore, MD. During his rounds, Captain Moore was talking with Private Sands and asking him about his family, school, and possible interest in a medical career. Tim was interested in the possibility of a medical career. Tim shared his encounter with a Dr. Young, who diagnosed his spider bite. Tim told how he was impressed with the doctor's analytical skills and ability to listen.

Private Timothy Sands said, "Dr. Moore, what do you find to be the most difficult part of this assignment?"

Without hesitation, Captain Moore said, "Triage. Surgery can be difficult, but at that moment, you are focused on the patient directly under your surgical care. Some surgeries can be more difficult than others, but all your efforts are focused on that one person. On the other hand, triage can become overwhelming. If you have twenty, thirty, or fifty people and maybe six operating tables, who goes first when you have fifteen who need immediate lifesaving surgery and, at that moment, only three surgeons available?"

Captain Moore could tell that Private Sands was contemplating the topic. He then said, "What have you found to be the most difficult part of your assignment?"

Private Sands said, "I had six patients on one dust off. I had to choose between clearing the airway of two patients. I had to choose."

Captain Moore and Private Sands had a moment of mutual respect, and the quietness was broken with a shout-out from a patient.

"Hey, Doc, can you get me some spaghetti with meatballs?"

Captain Moore was confused. He started to say something in response to the unusual request when Private Sands responded, "Lieutenant Fox, what did you do to earn a bed with clean sheets?"

Private Timothy Sands greeted Lieutenant Willis Fox with a handshake and introduced Captain Lloyd Moore.

Lieutenant Fox said, "Captain Moore, did you somehow recruit this newbie medic to your hospital?"

Captain Moore said, "I have not. However, I like the suggestion."

Lieutenant Fox said, "Forget it. I tried and failed. Apparently, a divisional commander by the name of Colonel Ron Buck thinks this young medic is a keeper. He has even earned himself an Army Commendation Medal having been in-country for less than a week."

Captain Moore said, "Is that so?"

Private Sands said, "I spent one night with Lieutenant Fox and his unit. He was kind enough to give me a meal of spaghetti with meatballs for breakfast."

Captain Moore said, "Okay, so the reference to Doc was out of respect to you as a medic?"

Lieutenant Fox said, "Yes, sir."

Captain Moore examined Lieutenant Fox's chart and handed it to Private Sands. Captain Moore then said, "Please look at this patient's chart, 'Doc.' Tell me what you think."

Private Sands looked at the chart and quickly determined that Lieutenant Fox had shrapnel removed from his leg with no expected long-term complications.

Private Sands said, "I think this patient should take two aspirin and call for the doctor tomorrow, if needed."

The three all laughed.

As the day progressed, Captain Moore and Private Sands had some detailed discussions on amputees. Tim was interested in these surgical procedures.

CHAPTER 25

COMBAT MEDIC BADGE

December in Vietnam brought about a series of transitions for Timothy Sands. The monsoon season was coming to an end. This led to an anticipation that battles would increase. An awards ceremony was conducted, and Tim was promoted to the rank of corporal. He was also awarded the Army Commendation Medal along with his combat medical badge. Corporal Jack Jackson was promoted to the rank of sergeant. These promotions put Tim in a Position of overseeing two new medics assigned to the 159th Medical Detachment. In addition, lieutenant Paul Robbins was assigned as the new flight commander for dust off 786, thus replacing Lieutenant Dennis Cordrey. Lieutenant Cordrey received his orders to go stateside as an early Christmas gift.

Corporal Timothy Sands greeted his new medics as they stepped off a C-123 transport plane. Private Charles Roundtree hailed from the great state of Maine. Private James McCoy called West Virginia his home. Tim was pleased his new medics represented the East Coast.

Christmas in Chu Chi brought about a major change in mood. Everyone was excited to hear that Bob Hope would be visiting the base camp. Several ground units were called back to the base if their operational mission allowed for the pause. Corporal Sands made arrangements for Privates Roundtree, McCoy, and himself to escort three of the wounded to the Bob Hope show. The entertainment provided by Bob Hope and his entourage changed the atmosphere for a few hundred war-torn soldiers for about two hours. However, the time of laughter, singing, and reflection would soon become a memory of a lifetime for those in attendance.

The New Year brought about several changes as well. However, the changes would prove to be less desirable. January ushered in the end of the monsoon season. This change in season meant that fighting would increase. In addition, the Vietnamese observed the lunar New Year, which they called the Tet. In the Tet of 1968, the North Vietnamese launched a major offensive attack in Saigon. The intelligence reports were beginning to anticipate another major Tet Offensive in the year 1969 as well.

On Wednesday, January 8, 1969, Corporal Tim Sands was helping with nursing duties at the hospital when he came upon a wounded medic in the recovery unit.

Tim introduced himself, "Good morning, Sergeant Driver. My name is Tim Sands."

Sergeant Driver replied, "Call me Bill."

"Okay, Bill. Is there anything I can get for you?"

"Yeah, a plane ticket out of here."

Tim said, "I think you've earned that ticket, but I was thinking of something more immediate, like a cup of iced water."

Bill didn't laugh, but he smiled and said, "You medics are all alike. You promise iced water to a dying soldier."

Tim said, "Speaking of medics, I thought it was against the Geneva Convention to shoot someone with a red cross on their helmet. How did you get in line for a ticket home?"

Bill said, "You don't understand. I was short enough to actually go home before today. My injuries and surgery have actually slowed down my departure."

Tim said, "If I were you, I wouldn't use the word *departure*. From what I can tell from your chart, you came close to traveling home in a body bag."

Bill said, "Yeah. I know."

Tim said, "Bill, where is home?"

"Home for me is New Jersey. And save the Jurseey jokes."

Tim said, "No kidding. I'm from Vineland, New Jersey.

Bill said, "Heck. We're neighbors. I'm from Camden."

"That's cool. Maybe someday we can get together and share a beer."

Bill said, "Well, at least, I got you to increase from a cup of iced water to a beer." Bill then started to laugh but stopped short when a burst of pain surged through his body. After the pain subsided, Bill said, "That wasn't fun."

Tim said, "Do you want me to get the nurse to give you some pain pills?"

Bill said, "No. I'm good. I just need to take it easy on the laughter. Maybe I will take you up on the cup of iced water."

Tim said, "No problem."

Tim returned with a bucket of ice and several cups and served iced water to several patients in the recovery unit.

Tim sat down next to Bill and said, "While I was getting the iced water, I checked on your plane ticket out of here. It looks like you have a ticket for stateside in two days."

Bill said, "I see you have a dust off patch. What are you doing in the hospital?"

Tim said, "I fly with dust off 768. I just volunteer in the hospital when I can."

Bill said, "You better be careful about volunteering."

Tim said, "I know. I spent one night with the Fourth Infantry Unit because I volunteered. I filled in for their medic because he was injured."

Bill said, "Do you want to volunteer for my unit in my absence?"

Tim said, "No, thank you. However, how did your unit make out when you were injured?"

"My unit was fortunate because my replacement was already in-country."

Tim asked, "Bill, do you mind if I ask you a question?"

"As long as you don't make me laugh."

Tim said, "No, it's a serious question. Since you have spent a year as a medic with a ground unit, what did you find to be the hardest thing about your job?"

Bill thought for a few minutes and then said, "Death is hard, but that's out of our control. Serious injuries are hard, but good training enables us to do the best we can in the moment. However, you can't imagine what it's like to run out of medical supplies. Our medic's bag can only carry so much. It's hard, really hard, to run out of tourniquets or morphine or ventilation equipment or bandages."

Tim said, "Bill, I'm glad you told me this. I've seen makeshift tourniquets and undersized bandages, and I never considered how hard it must be to run short of needed medical supplies. It's been a pleasure meeting you. Can we make an effort to get together back in the States?"

Bill offered his hand and said, "Yes, I would like that."

CHAPTER 26

In early February 1969, enemy activity accelerated in the area of Da Nang. On February 22, 1969, one year after the original Tet Offensive in 1968, the Northern Vietnamese launched a massive attack on military targets near Saigon, Da Nang, Long Binh Post, and the Chu Chi base camp. On February 26, sappers destroyed nine CH-47 Chinook helicopters on the Chu Chi base camp airport tarmac. Sappers are enemy demolition experts who infiltrate security boundaries with the intent to destroy important targets. On March 10, 1969, sapper squads broke through the Chu Chi base camp perimeter and attempted to destroy helicopters.

During these battles, Corporal Timothy Sands demonstrated courage, medical expertise, and earned a much-deserved recommendation for the award of a Bronze Star. With only six months in country, Tim was recommended to appear before a promotions board for consideration of a promotion to the rank of sergeant.

The fighting along the Cambodia border was accelerating, and Corporal Sands began to see an increased number of wounded with makeshift bandages and tourniquets. He recalled his conversation with Sergeant Bill Driver. He thought about the possibility of a medic with a shortage of medical supplies. Tim decided to do something.

Corporal Timothy Sands went to the medical supply office and asked for a complete medic's bag. The supply sergeant had a question for Corporal Sands.

Staff Sergeant Lester LaTour said, "Corporal Sands, our records indicate you have been issued a medic's bag. Did you somehow lose your bag?"

Tim replied, "No, Sergeant LaTour. I still have my bag. I just want a spare in case a ground unit medic needs additional medical supplies."

Staff Sergeant LaTour said, "Request denied."

Tim started to say something, but Staff Sergeant LaTour cut him off.

"I'm not here to provide spare supplies. I'm having a hard time just keeping up with the current high level of demands."

Tim decided on another course of action.

*****

The promotions board was announced, and Corporal Timothy Sands was one of three candidates under consideration. Captain Douglas Alexander, MD, Master Sergeant Jon Knox, and Staff Sergeant Lester LaTour all comprised the promotions board.

Captain Alexander said, "Corporal Sands, this board has been tasked with the obligation to determine if you should be promoted to the rank of sergeant (E-5). Please relax, answer our questions, and add any additional information you feel would be beneficial for our consideration."

"Yes, sir."

Captain Alexander continued, "Corporal Sands, I have reviewed your training records, your evaluations, and received some strong recommendations from several doctors and nurses from the Twelfth Hospital. Am I correct to understand that you volunteer at the hospital several days a week?"

"Yes, sir. I do volunteer when I can."

Captain Alexander continued, "Corporal Sands, I am being told that when you do volunteer at the hospital, you always check in first with the doctor assigned at triage. Why triage?"

"Sir, I understand that triage can become an overwhelmingly difficult assignment. If I can be of any help to the doctor in charge, then that's what I want to do."

Master Sergeant Knox said, "Corporal Sands, I understand you were awarded the Army Commendation Medal having only been in-country for less than a week. I am correct that you volunteered to join the Fourth Infantry Unit as a plot to leave the 159th Medical Detachment?"

"Master Sergeant Knox, with all due respect, I did not volunteer as a plot to leave the 159th. During that mission, I was an extra medic on a medevac extraction. The medic assigned to the Fourth Infantry Unit was severely injured. It didn't make sense for two medics to fly away when the ground unit didn't have any medic. My flight commander approved of my providing medical assistance to the ground unit."

Master Sergeant Knox said, "It is my understanding you have been recommended for the awarding of a Bronze Star for your actions during the Tet Offensive. Am I correct with this information?"

"Master Sergeant Knox, the possibility of my receiving a Bronze Star is humbling."

Staff Sergeant Lester LaTour asked, "Corporal Sands, did you come to my supply unit and request a spare medic's bag?"

"Yes, Sergeant LaTour, I did."

"Did I deny your request for a spare medic's bag?"

"Yes, Sergeant Latour, you did."

"It is my understanding that you have recently gained a reputation for throwing a bag of extra medical supplies to ground unit medics. Corporal Sands, are you skimming off medical supplies in order to pass these supplies to ground unit medics?"

"Staff Sergeant LaTour, I am not skimming off medical supplies. I sent a request to my parents to send me over-the-counter medical supplies and pillowcases marked with a red cross. My parents took my request to our church. As a result, I have been receiving a box of medical supplies about once a week. If a ground unit has a large number of casualties, I can only imagine the ground unit medic could use additional medical supplies. These medical supplies are generic bandages, over-the-counter antiseptics, splints, ace bandages, tourniquets, wound packing gauze, and more importantly, cookies and candy. I have not been involved in skimming off any authorized medical supplies."

Captain Alexander said, "Corporal Sands, it is common knowledge that Colonel Ron Buck is being transferred stateside and we will soon have a change of command ceremony. We understand the change of command will result in new leadership under the command of Colonel Jacob Shappell. Colonel Ron Buck sent this promotions board a note in reference to your possible promotion. This note reads, 'Doctor Al, I understand you are considering Corporal Timothy Sands for a promotion to sergeant. I believe your promotions board will find everything in order for such a promotion. Don't delay in your deliberations, because I want to include the promotion and presentation of the Bronze Star to Sergeant Timothy Sands prior to the change of command ceremony.' Corporal Sands, it sounds like our divisional commander not only has an interest in your promotion but also believes everything to be in order. How do you believe this promotions board should consider such a note from our divisional commander?"

Corporal Timothy Sands said, "Sir, with all due respect, I recommend you don't delay in your deliberations."

They all laughed.

Thursday, April 10, 1969—countdown 142 days

Colonel Ron Buck made some kind comments about me in his change of command ceremony today. He felt pride in having soldiers like me under his command. He promoted me to the rank of sergeant (E-5) and presented me with the Bronze Star. I'm not sure how I feel about the Bronze Star.

The Army uses locals to do some work on our base camp. We had someone who worked in our mess hall set up a bomb behind the food tray rack. When one of our guys pulled out a food tray, the bomb blew up. This event took me back to Cooper's Camp when a spider bit me. Doctor Young said check your sleeping bag and boots for spiders and snakes. I need to be careful, but I can't get paranoid. I understand fear can become problematic, as we get short.

Good night.
Overcomer

CHAPTER 27

Dust off 768 was returning from a medevac, and Lieutenant Paul Robbins spoke to Sergeant Timothy Sands on the intercom. "Sands, I just got a call from headquarters. When we land, you are to report to the divisional commander. Apparently, Colonel Jacob Shappell wants to see you."

Tim said, "I'm not sure I like the sounds of this."

Lieutenant Robbins said, "Sergeant Sands, just for your information, if the good colonel tries to reassign you, I am going to put up a fight."

Tim responded, "Commander, I hope that's not on his mind."

Tim reported to the office of the divisional commander.

"Sir, Sergeant Sands reporting as directed."

Colonel Shappell returned the salute and said, "Stand at ease, Sergeant."

"Thank you, sir."

Colonel Shappell said, "Sergeant Sands, when I met with Colonel Ron Buck to discuss the change of command ceremony he was determined to include your promotion and the presentation of the Bronze Star to you before he relinquished his command. I am sure you could tell by his comments that Colonel Buck has a high opinion of you as a soldier."

"Yes, sir."

"Sergeant Sands, what you didn't know was our detailed discussion about your future. Colonel Ron Buck was working on a plan for several weeks and asked me to follow up with his plan. It's been a month since we have been working on this project."

"Sir, I don't understand where this is going."

"I know I have been a little evasive. Sergeant Sands, I just received approval to offer you an appointment to West Point. Colonel Buck began this process, and we just received approval along with a recommendation from your congressman for this appointment."

"Sir, I am certainly honored and surprised by such an appointment."

"I'm sure this is a lot to think about. However, Colonel Buck fought through a bunch of bureaucracy because he felt strongly that you represent the best of our Army. I have only been in this position for a month, but I have been impressed with the comments by my staff on your behalf. If you should accept this appointment, you would receive a first-class education and serve in the Army as an officer. I believe this would be beneficial to you and definitely favorable to the ranks of the Army. I also need to advise you of the potential time line for this appointment. Today is May 12. Your in-country tour of duty ends on September 10. The only way for you to begin your plebe year in July of this year is to terminate your active in-country duty early. This entire process would not have been possible had we not received approval for this plan by my superior, General Benjamin Krouse. I am prepared to cut orders for you to leave on June 2, take a thirty-day leave at home, and report to West Point on July 2."

"Wow! This is a lot to think about."

"Sergeant Sands, I understand this is a big decision. Your reputation has moved a lot of people to develop a plan that reflects well on you. Why don't you take a couple of days to consider this appointment? Let's say you get back to me by Friday."

"Sir, thank you. I will give you an answer by Friday."

Timothy Sands took a long walk back to his hooch. He lay on his bed for an hour, thinking of all the challenges and opportunities he was facing. Tim had developed a good relationship with the divisional chaplain. Tim had worked with the chaplain on several occasions in the hospital. Tim spent a long time in conversation and prayer with the chaplain.

Sergeant Timothy Sands reported to the office of Colonel Jacob Shappell on Friday, May 16. Tim advised the colonel that he would accept the appointment to West Point. Colonel Shappell called for Captain Dale Wade, 159th Air Medevac Company commander, and Lieutenant Paul Robbins, dust off 768-flight commander, to report to his office.

When Captain Wade and Lieutenant Robbins reported to Colonel Shappell's office, they were curious as to why Sergeant Timothy Sands was in the office.

Colonel Shappell said, "Gentlemen, I have called you here to tell you Sergeant Timothy Sands will be leaving your unit."

Lieutenant Robbins was quick to respond. "Sir, if I may speak in objection."

Colonel Shappell cut him off. "No, Lieutenant, you may not speak in objection, because you didn't give me time to finish telling you why Sergeant Sands is leaving your unit. Colonel Ron Buck and I have been working on a plan to obtain an appointment to West Point for Sergeant Timothy Sands. I am pleased to report that I am cutting orders for Sergeant Sands to leave on June 2, he will have a thirty-day leave, and report to West Point on July 2."

Lieutenant Robbins was quick to shake hands and congratulate Tim. He said, "Colonel Shappell, I withdraw my objection. I was ready to fight against any transfer, but this is great news."

Captain Wade also shook hands with Tim and offered his congratulations as well.

Tim said, "Colonel Shappell, thank you for all the work you did to make this possible. Would it be possible for me to have an address to send a letter to Colonel Ron Buck?"

"Certainly."

That night, Tim wrote three letters. Tim thanked Colonel Ron Buck for his confidence and the work the colonel did to make this appointment possible. Tim's second letter was to his parents. The third letter was to his best friend, Brett Corson.

CHAPTER 28

Lieutenant Alyssa Wilson was checking Sergeant Timothy Sands's blood pressure as he began to awaken from his third surgery. Alyssa has been Tim's nurse for over two months since his arrival at the Walter Reed Hospital in Bethesda, Maryland. The two have developed a friendship that Tim describes as "hopeful" if Alyssa could ever accept his disabilities.

Alyssa said, "Well, good afternoon, Tim. I was beginning to wonder if you were going to sleep throughout my shift."

Tim's response was slow, and his speech a little slurred, but he managed to say, "So I'm dead. I see an angel."

Alyssa said, "Indeed, an angel who is about to give you a needle."

Tim smiled but didn't respond.

Alyssa said, "Rest up. I'll check back with you after my shift." Alyssa gave him a kiss on his forehead.

Tim touched his lips with his good hand. He said, "You missed."

Alyssa said, "Nice try, but you haven't even taken me out on one date yet."

Tim smiled and drifted back to sleep.

Later in the day, Dr. Anthony Compari entered Tim's hospital room and greeted the small gathering of Tim's parents, sister Sandra, and off-duty nurse Alyssa Wilson. Dr. Compari said, "Sergeant Sands, do you mind if we discuss some things with everyone in the room?"

"Sir, please proceed. This is my support group."

"Okay. I will begin with the good news. I believe you will be able to regain most of the use of your left hand. The bad news is that we were unable to save your third and fourth fingers. As I told you before surgery, those two fingers sustained the most crushing damage, and it was unlikely that we could save them."

Tim said, "What about my leg? Is there any good news?"

Dr. Compari said, "I hope you will accept this as good news. We were able to finalize the amputation below the knee. This means you will likely be able to gain some reasonable mobility with a prosthetic. What we did today will allow for stability and flexibility with the full use of your knee. I know we discussed the loss of your lower leg and two fingers prior to this surgery, but, in reality, what we did today allows for the best use of your remaining hand and leg. You may need to relearn how to type with two less digits. However, you will be able to type. You may also need to adjust to walking on a stick. However, you will be able to walk. Sergeant Sands, as a combat medic, I know you have observed some terrible injuries. You know that sometimes we need to put our situation into perspective. Be thankful you won't need to depend on someone to feed you, and be thankful you will not be confined to a wheelchair for the remainder of your life."

"I am thankful. I was the only survivor of our helicopter being shot down. What about my loss of memory? I don't remember anything about the crash or anything about my medevac."

Dr. Compari replied, "Your loss of memory is directly related to the trauma you suffered to the head. You certainly suffered a concussion, but I think your flight helmet saved your life. I would consider your failure to remember the crash as another blessing."

"I don't know why God allowed me to live, but I have to believe that my life will not be defined by my injuries. I have been blessed."

Dr. Compari said, "Well said. I will stop by tomorrow to change your bandages. I want to see how everything looks." He then turned to Tim's family and said, "Sergeant Sands is fortunate to have you all as his support group. I can only deal with the medical aspects of his physical healing. You all will need to help him with the emotional and mental challenges and his ability to tolerate and overcome the pain."

Margaret gave Dr. Compari a hug and said, "Thank you for your medical skills and compassion."

Robert and Sandra shook the doctor's hand.

Dr. Compari stood in front of Alyssa Wilson and said, "Lieutenant Wilson, are you here in support of Sergeant Sands as his nurse or as his friend?"

She simply said, "Yes, sir."

He said, "Good. Please plan on being here tomorrow. I want you to assist me with the changing of his bandages."

"Yes, sir. I will be here."

Dr. Compari turned to Tim and said, "For now, you need to rely on the pain medication. We need your body to heal. We will reduce the drugs later."

Tim said, "I understand."

Dr. Compari left the room. Tim's family commented on how much they appreciated the doctor. Alyssa said, "Dr. Compari is considered to be the best surgeon we have. Most staff would vote for him as being the doctor of the year."

Sandra noticed that Tim was getting sleepy eyes. She said, "I think we all need to leave. Timmy needs to get some sleep."

Margaret said, "Timothy, I brought your journal and the pillowcase you requested."

Tim took his journal and set it on the tray table. He took the neatly folded pillowcase and laid it over his left arm and closed his eyes.

On the following day, Dr. Anthony Compari and Lieutenant Alyssa Wilson entered Tim's room with a cart loaded down with medications and bandages. Tim was writing in his journal. He put down his journal and said, "Good morning. Do you have my discharge papers?"

Dr. Compari replied, "Lieutenant Wilson, remind me to realign some of his nerves to inflict pain when the patient says something that is irresponsible."

Alyssa laughed and replied, "I was thinking the same thing when the patient flirts with other nurses."

Tim said, "Okay, I surrender. No additional pain."

Dr. Compari said, "Seriously, how is your pain level today?"

Tim said, "Sitting here I'm feeling about a seven out of ten. However, I anticipate the level will go up once you two start poking around."

Dr. Compari studied Tim's chart and then said, "Okay, let's start with a shot for pain. I don't want your pain to increase, because we will make things a little more uncomfortable."

Dr. Compari and Lieutenant Wilson then began by unwrapping Tim's leg. Dr. Compari looked closely at the stump and cleaned the area of surgery. They asked Tim to move his leg and slightly bend his knee. Any movement was painful, but Tim was able to move his leg and bend his knee, ever so slightly and slowly. The doctor and nurse worked together to rewrap Tim's stump. They examined Tim's hand and again asked for movement in his wrist and thumb. Tim was unable to move his two remaining fingers. The examination and rewrapping were completed, and Dr. Compari said, "Sergeant Sands, I'm pleased with everything. I'm not concerned with the lack of movement in your fingers. We need to give them some more time for healing."

Dr. Compari started writing instructions on Tim's chart. He said, "Lieutenant Wilson, starting tomorrow sergeant Sands should be sitting up with his leg elevated for one hour in the a.m. and one hour in the p.m." He then turned to Tim and said, "Sergeant Sands, under no circumstances are to get out of bed without assistance. Is that understood?"

Tim said, "Yes, sir. I understand."

Tim then opened a pillowcase with a red cross painted in the center. Tim said, "Dr. Compari, would you kindly sign this pillowcase?"

Dr. Compari said, "Obviously, this pillowcase has some significance. I would be honored to sign it. Would you tell me the story behind it?"

Tim explained the origin of the medic's supply bag. Tim said, "Apparently, when our helicopter was shot down, the medic who saved my life signed this pillowcase and tied it around my good arm. He signed it on the top-left-hand corner." Tim pointed to the signature, which read,

To Sergeant Sands, candy man. Godspeed.
From Corporal Don Beauregard.

"When I was medevaced to the Twelfth Hospital, the hospital staff took care of the pillowcase. Someone from the hospital gathered signatures, and in the center of the red cross, someone neatly printed

'Dust off #786, mayday—May 26, 1969, Lt. Paul Robbins, flight commander, KIA, WO2 Mike Porter, Pilot, KIA, Sgt. Rob Gott, crew chief, KIA.' The other signatures on the pillowcase are fellow soldiers, medics, doctors, and nurses. I would like to have you sign this pillowcase as someone responsible for saving my life."

Dr. Anthony Compari signed the pillowcase. Alyssa Wilson was standing in the background and wiped tears from her eyes.

Later in the week, Alyssa came rushing into Tim's room and said, "Guess what, big shot.'

Tim said, "Okay, I give up. What's up?"

"You are having some company today. Therefore, you need to shave and make yourself presentable."

"And for whom should I shave?"

"Oh, just the president of the United States and a couple of tagalong generals and some newspeople."

Tim said, "And why exactly should I shave? If I am having visitors, I would like to have something to wear beside this stupid gown with an open-air backside. Can you tell me why patients need to wear these stupid gowns?"

Alyssa said, "Tim, you need to shave. I will get you a regular gown that ties in the front."

Activity around the hospital increased. Men in dark suits were walking around looking in rooms and opening doors. Tim said, "Apparently, these secret service guys are not taking any chances. Hey, how did you hear about all this since today is your day off?"

Alyssa said, "One of my coworkers called me."

Tim said, "What are the chances that the president will actually come to my room?"

Alyssa said, "Tim, I'm being told he is coming to see you."

President Jeffrey Adams and his entourage entered Tim's room. The room was instantly filled with an interesting quiet. President Adams first greeted and shook hands with Alyssa. He then greeted Tim and said, "Sergeant Sands, I understand you sustained your injuries while serving as a medic in Vietnam. I also understand you were the lone survivor in the incident as your helicopter was shot down."

"Sir, yes, sir."

"Sergeant Timothy Sands, I am honored to present you with the Purple Heart in recognition of the injuries you sustained as a member of our armed services."

An aide handed the Purple Heart to President Adams. He then pinned the medal on Tim's chest. The aide then handed the citation and the empty Purple Heart box to Alyssa.

Then a general stepped forward and stood alongside the president. The general said, "President Adams, we have another situation that needs to be brought to your attention. Sergeant Timothy Sands was accepted as a cadet to the United States Military Academy at West Point, and he had orders to appear at our premier military academy on July 2, 1969. Sergeant Timothy Sands failed to appear as ordered."

President Adams said, "So apparently, Sergeant Sands was injured, and his orders were not amended. To me, this sounds like his unit commander failed to amend this soldier's orders."

The general said, "Mr. President, the unit commander did submit a change of orders for Sergeant Sands. May I have your permission to read these orders?"

President Adams said, "Proceed."

The general said, "As the divisional commander for the 159th Medical Detachment, 25th Infantry Division, serving in the Republic of Vietnam, I, hereby, issue a promotion for Sergeant Timothy Sands to the rank of second lieutenant. This battlefield commission is effective May 26, 1969. Signed Colonel Jacob Shappell."

An aide handed one golden lieutenant's bar to President Adams and one bar to Alyssa Wilson. The aide assisted with posing President Adams on one side of Tim and Alyssa Wilson on the other side, and news photographers began snapping pictures of Timothy Sands being pinned on the shoulders of a dark-blue bathrobe.

President Adams said, "Congratulations, Lieutenant Timothy Sands."

Tim said, "President Adams, I am extremely thankful for these honors. With all due respect, could I ask you, as my commander in chief, to sign something?"

"Certainly."

Tim removed the pillowcase from his nightstand. Tim then unfolded the pillowcase to reveal the red cross and several signatures. The news photographers started taking pictures and began pushing for a better photo advantage. President Adams merely raised his hand. and the newspeople came to a halt.

President Adams looked closely at the signatures and inscription in the midst of the red cross. He then remarked, "So it appears your helicopter was shot down on May 26. Your crew members all died in the crash. Your promotion was effective on the day your pilot called for a May Day, which happens to be Memorial Day as well. Please tell me the story of the pillowcase."

Tim recited the story of the pillowcase.

The commander in chief signed the pillowcase and expressed his deepest gratitude.

The next day, newspapers across the country ran with front-page stories of the lack of medical supplies for frontline medics in the Vietnam War. The news photos showed an injured medic at the Walter Reed Hospital with a Purple Heart and golden lieutenant's bars, but the story and headlines focused on donated Band-Aids for combat medics. Tim's memorial to dust off 786 was effectively reduced to a poster for war critics.

Part 4

The Adventures in Marriage

Actually, the best gift you could have given
her was a lifetime of adventures.

—Lewis Carroll

CHAPTER 29

Tim was progressing nicely with his healing. He was allowed to travel around the hospital in a wheelchair, so the time was right for him to make some important plans for his future. He had a private conversation with Dr. Anthony Compari and received permission to proceed with phase one of his plan.

Alyssa was scheduled to be off on Monday, September 1. Tim knew she would visit with him around 11:00 a.m. When Alyssa arrived, she was pleased to see that Tim was dressed, sitting in a wheelchair and holding a bouquet of flowers.

Tim greeted her with a smile, presented her with the flowers, and asked, "Will you allow me to take you out on a date?"

Alyssa said, "Just what do you have in mind? A trip down to the hospital cafeteria?"

Tim said, "Nope, we are going out. Before you ask, I have permission."

Alyssa said, "Okay, let's go."

Tim said, "The only problem is you need to drive."

Alyssa said, "So I open the car passenger door for you, and I drive. Am I expected to pay for our first date as well?"

Tim said, "That's not a bad idea."

Alyssa playfully punched him on the shoulder and said, "If I'm paying, we are going to the hospital cafeteria."

Tim said, "No way. I'm ready for a steak dinner with a beautiful girl. Let's go."

Tim was able to maneuver himself into the passenger side of Alyssa's car. She folded up the wheelchair and put it into the trunk, and together they travelled to a BBQ steak house. This was the first time Tim had been out in the public for close to a year. The two had a great meal and an enjoyable time together.

After lunch, Tim said, "We have one more stop."

Alyssa said, "Okay, point the way."

Tim directed Alyssa to the apartment complex across the street from his hospital. Tim said, "Come on, I want to show you my new apartment."

"For real?"

"Yes. I have approval to move into an apartment. I still need treatments and therapy at the hospital. However, Dr. Compari gave his approval for me to live here as long as I didn't skip any appointments."

Tim was pleased to show off his new freedom space. He said, "I look forward to our having some home-cooked dinners together."

Alyssa didn't say anything, but she bent over and proceeded to kiss Tim on the lips. He said, "You didn't miss this time."

She said, "Shut up." They kissed again and embraced for a long time.

Alyssa asked, "Are you sure you can handle the responsibilities of maintaining your own apartment?"

Tim said, "Realistically, I will need some help. My sister Sandra is coming down to live with me for a while. She will help with the cleaning, shopping, and cooking. However, her main objective is to help me learn how to do these things. I am trying to be hopeful that things will improve when I finally learn how to walk with my prosthetic leg."

Alyssa said, "Tim, let's not 'try' to be hopeful that things will improve. Let us determine together that we will be victorious."

CHAPTER 30

Over four months, Tim and Alyssa developed a loving relationship. Tim's sister, Sandra, was a great help to Tim during this period of time. Sandra and Alyssa also developed a friendship, and they liked shopping together and often enjoyed a girls' night out. The threesome found a church, which they felt was spiritually uplifting and provided a circle of friends who shared in like interests.

Tim was fitted with a prosthetic leg and was doing remarkably well with his mobility. As Christmas was approaching, Tim had a long conversation with Dr. Anthony Compari, and it was agreed that Tim was ready to move on to the next phase of his recovery. Dr. Compari was prepared to recommend Tim's medical discharge from active-duty status. Tim would hang up his uniform effective January 1, 1970. Tim would remain in medical care through the Veterans Administration (VA), but he would no longer require the services of the Walter Reed Hospital. His medical care would be available anywhere in the country through the VA.

Tim made plans to take Alyssa out for dinner at the same BBQ steak house where they went on their first date. After dinner, Tim asked Alyssa to drive them to the Lincoln Memorial. It was a cold evening, but Tim was determined to walk hand in hand with Alyssa up the steps of the memorial. On the steps of this grand memorial, overlooking the majestic sights of our nation's capital, Tim knelt down and said, "Alyssa, I love you with all of my heart. I cannot promise you anything beyond my love and devotion, but will you marry me?" He then presented her with a ring and slid it on her ring finger.

Alyssa helped Tim stand and placed her left hand on the side of his face and said, "Yes. And I love you with all my heart as well." The two kissed and embraced for a long time.

Tim made his way down the steps and back to his wheelchair. Alyssa stood beside him as they enjoyed the Christmas lights gleaming throughout the capital.

Tim said, "At least we can save some money on the wedding."

"How?"

"We don't need to buy me a wedding ring." Tim held up his left hand with a missing ring finger.

Alyssa said, "Don't count on it. You still have six fingers and two thumbs."

They laughed.

Alyssa said, "Let's go. I'm getting cold."

Tim said, "Yes, dear."

Alyssa said, "I love hearing you say those two words."

Tim replied, "I'm looking forward to you saying the two words 'I do.'"

When they got to Alyssa's car, they sat for a while in the warmth provided by the car's heater. Alyssa said, "We need to go to your apartment. I need to call my mother and sister."

Tim didn't tell Alyssa that Sandra and he had arranged a combined family Christmas party. Those in attendance were his father Robert, mother Margaret, and brother John and his fiancée, Janice Strauss. Sandra also arranged for Alyssa's family to share in the occasion as well. Alyssa's father Terry, mother Judi, and sister Vicki were also included in the celebration. Sandra made arrangements for dinner and overnight accommodations for everyone. Only Sandra knew of Tim's plan for the big announcement of Tim and Alyssa's engagement.

When Tim and Alyssa arrived at Tim's apartment, she was surprised and thrilled to show off her ring. Everyone was excited about the engagement. The talk of wedding plans alternated between John and Janice's plans and Tim and Alyssa's plans. Margaret was excited about gaining two new daughters. However, as the evening began to drift late into the night, the planned Christmas celebration was called to an end with a Wilson family tradition. Terry Wilson read the biblical account of Jesus's birth from Luke 2. They ended the evening by sharing in a birthday cake for Jesus.

The Sands family traveled home to New Jersey early Christmas morning. They wanted to get home for a Christmas Day dinner with Margaret's side of the family. The Wilsons wanted to have breakfast with Tim and Alyssa before they took off for their home in Virginia. During breakfast, Terry Wilson made Tim a job offer.

Terry said, "Tim, I don't know what you have in mind for your future, but I have an offer you may want to consider. As you know, I have a printing business. My daughters have made it clear they have no interest in taking on the family business. Vicki is consumed with flying and anything related to aviation. That's okay with me. I want for her whatever she wants. Alyssa is happy in her nursing career, and that's great. However, over the years, I have always purchased the best equipment available, and typically, I only get about 30 percent of the output my equipment is capable of handling. I want to expand my business. I need someone to help me out. If you were interested, I would love to bring you into the family business."

Tim said, "Mr. Wilson, I really appreciate the offer. I'm not yet ready to make those kinds of decisions. How long do I have to consider your offer?"

Terry said, "Call me Dad or Terry or sir or Alyssa's old man, but please drop the 'Mr. Wilson' stuff. I will not push you into any time frame. If you ever think it's a closed door, just say so. If it's a yes, then I will accept any time frame you can work into. Your health and recovery are most important. I will work with any adjustments you need to accommodate your physical conditions."

"Thank you, Dad. I need to talk with Alyssa first."

Judi said, "Now that's a smart man."

They all laughed.

That evening, Tim and Alyssa and Sandra were sitting together in Tim's apartment, tired from all the Christmas celebrations. Sandra said, "Tim, I'm going to bed, but I want you to know I think it's now time for me to go home. You are doing well with the apartment. You don't need me to care for you, and it's probably time for you and Alyssa to make decisions about your next move. For whatever it's worth, I think you should seriously consider the job offer from

Alyssa's dad. He's not just offering you a job. He's opening the door for a business opportunity. Just saying."

"I know. Thanks, Sandra."

After Sandra went to bed, Tim and Alyssa had a long discussion about their immediate future.

Alyssa said, "Tim, Sandra's right. My dad has a very successful business. I know he's disappointed that neither Vicki nor I are interested in working in the printing business. However, my dad has made a good living, and his plans for the future could result in the proverbial gold mine. As for me, should you decide to take the job offer from Dad, I will gladly move back home. I'm not worried about work. I know I can find a nursing position at home. I love living in the Shenandoah Valley region of Virginia, and I think you will as well."

Tim said, "I certainly do not know anything about the printing business, but I feel that your dad is willing to give me some time to learn. I think your father will also give me time to adapt to my physical challenges."

Tim seemed to drift off into another world.

Alyssa said, "When you get back, let me know where you went."

Tim said, "Sorry. I was thinking of something I want us to do before we get married."

Alyssa said, "And."

"I have a list of soldiers with whom I served. I want us to visit with their families and in some cases visit a gravesite. With your approval, I would like to invite some of these families to our wedding. These men are my brothers."

"Thank you for including me in these visits."

Tim said, "I think I will call your father tomorrow for a little chat. Then you and I can start making plans to move."

Alyssa was holding Tim's right hand while sitting next to him on the couch. She raised his hand and kissed it.

Tim said, "You have the unique ability to miss with your kisses." He then touched his lips.

"I didn't miss. I just marked the ring finger of your right hand for a wedding ring."

Tim pulled her into an embrace and kissed her.

CHAPTER 31

Tim initially moved into an apartment on the outer edge of Harrisonburg, Virginia. Alyssa moved back home with her parents and sister. Tim's first day on the job at the Standard Printing Company was primarily an introduction to the workers and a walk through the printing plant. In practically every introduction, Tim would greet the worker and then say, "Please show me what you are doing." All the workers knew Tim was Terry's future son-in-law. They also knew he was coming into the business with zero experience. The workers didn't care. They were happy, and Terry treated all his workers with respect and offered reasonable pay and generous benefits. The general opinion of the workers was, if the boss wanted to bring in his new son-in-law, so be it.

Tim had an interesting conversation with Justin at the paper cutter. Justin was operating a large guillotine paper cutter. Justin said, "It's very important to place the paper in the proper position, and then both hands must be on the two safety grips before the cutter would function by activation of a foot switch."

Tim held up his left hand and said, "Justin, maybe our customers will think I was careless in the use of a paper cutter."

Justin said, "Yeah, you may want to use that as your story. No one is going to be interested in your combat injuries."

Tim asked, "Are you a vet?"

Justin said, "Yeah. But it's not a popular topic, so don't think it's something important to talk about."

Tim said, "I know."

Tim then proceeded to a discussion with a Greg as he operated the main dot matrix printer. Tim was curious about a large empty space next to the printer.

Tim said, "Greg, why is there so much empty space between your printer and the tables with paper and supplies?"

Greg said, "We just created that space for a brand-new state-of-the-art printer. The new printer will be a new laser printer. It's the newest printer on the market, and Mr. Wilson has ordered one. We will be one of the first printing companies to have such a printer. From what I understand, the quality and output from the laser printer will allow us to do some amazing things. I'm not even sure we know how much this new printer will improve our quality and volume of output."

Tim was tired from standing. He didn't want to use a wheel-chair at work, but the first day was proving to be a physical challenge. Tim soon found that the best location for learning about the printing business was by sitting with Sandi North. Sandi had about twenty years of experience and served as the office manager. Sandi's duties included sales, purchasing, accounts payable, and payroll. Tim learned from Sandi how to estimate printing jobs. Sandi convinced Tim that his best contribution to the business would be sales. The company had first-class equipment and skilled workers. What they needed was an increase in business.

Tim spoke with Terry, and it was agreed that Tim should spend quality time on the road as a salesperson. Tim would seek to generate new customers. Vicki Wilson made an offer to serve as Tim's driver. And when necessary, Vicki would fly Tim to distant locations in an effort to generate new customers.

Tim was in his apartment when the new washer and dryer that he had ordered were delivered. The deliverymen installed the appliances and made sure everything was in working order. When the deliverymen were ready to leave, they requested Tim's signature. Tim signed the appropriate receipt, and one deliveryman handed Tim a pack of documents pertaining to the new appliances. Tim sat for a while, looking through the booklets on instructions for installation, repairs, and limitations on warranties pertaining to these appliances. Given his training by Sandi, Tim thought about these documents. He began to analyze how much it would cost to print them. He then began to wonder if he could obtain a contract from a big-name appliance manufacturer for printing these documents. Tim then spent the next two hours developing a cost analysis for such a project and made several phone calls.

When Sandi arrived at work, she was surprised to see Tim sitting in the lobby. Sandi said, "Tim, is everything okay?"

Tim said, "Yes. Everything is fine. I just need you to review a cost analysis I developed on a potential printing job."

Sandi said, "Okay, I just need to open the shop and make coffee."

Tim said, "I already did those things for you. I need you to look at this proposal right away because I have an appointment and I don't want to make a big mistake."

Sandi unlocked her office and sat at her desk. Tim soon followed with a fresh cup of coffee for Sandi. He then handed her a printing proposal for King Spin Appliances. Sandi looked at the proposal. "Oh my. This is a big project. Do you think you can land such a contract?"

Tim said, "Yes. If my numbers are correct. That's why I need your approval."

Sandi took a sip of coffee and said, "Let me look at this proposal." She shooed Tim away with a wave of her hand.

Sandi soon called Tim on the telephone intercom system.

"I'm on my way."

Sandi handed Tim the proposal and said, "You did a fine analysis. I wrote a few notes for your consideration. Your profit margin doesn't allow for much negotiation. I would suggest you raise the total package by 5 percent. If you are pushed into a reduction, you can drop by 2.5 percent. I wouldn't drop any lower unless the total number of packages doubles."

Tim said, "Thank you. Let's see if this works."

Two days later, Tim stopped by Sandi's office. He said, "Sandi, I was able to meet with a second vice president for King Spin Appliances. He said no."

Sandi said, "Doesn't hurt to try."

Tim said, "I'm going to try the same thing with the television company from which I just purchased a big TV."

Sandi said, "Doesn't hurt to try."

Tim said, "And then I am going to try an airline company for the printing of those instruction cards on plane evacuations. And then I am going to try an automobile manufacturing company."

Sandi laughed and shooed him away with her hand.

CHAPTER 32

Tim and Alyssa were making progress on their wedding plans. They were meeting with their pastor for premarital counseling. Tim was living in the home they had chosen to rent. Tim was purchasing the necessary appliances, fixing things up, and painting rooms for their eventual home together.

As part of Tim's goal, they were slowly visiting with the families and graves of those with whom Tim served. One of the more pleasant visits was Tim's meeting with someone he never formally met. Tim and Alyssa visited with the former corporal Don Beauregard. Don was the medic who treated Tim at the crash site of dust off 786. Don was responsible for saving Tim's life and probably responsible for saving Tim's leg by correctly applying the tourniquet in a timely fashion. Don and Tim had never met; however, while Don was treating Tim at the crash site, he knew of Sergeant Sands' reputation of providing medical supplies and candy in a pillowcase marked with a red cross. Don treated Tim and signed the pillowcase, which he had received and tied it to Tim's arm, hoping Tim would someday realize how the medical supplies and candy were appreciated by his fellow medics. During this visit, Tim wanted to thank Don as the medic who saved his life. Tim also wanted to ask a few questions about the circumstances of the dust off 786's crash.

Tim said, "Don, I was never told what caused the crash of our helicopter."

Don asked, "So you don't have any memory of the crash?"

"No."

Don was slow to answer. He then said, "Tim, if you have no memory of the crash, then let's just leave it that way. If I begin to describe things, you will just ask for more and more details. Besides,

137

I've done my best to forget things I can't forget, so why should I fill your head with crap that isn't even there?"

Alyssa said, "Don, your compassion is appreciated."

Don was quick to answer. "Speaking of compassion, Tim, you are the only person that went out of your way to find me and to thank me as the medic who treated them."

Tim said, "Just one more question."

Don said, "You can ask your question. I may or may not answer it."

Tim said, "Was it raining the day you rescued me?"

Don said, "No rain. I know that for a fact. That seems like an unusual question. Why ask about rain?"

Tim said, "I have a recurring dream. I have never been able to connect the dream with anything. It's a disturbing dream, and it is somehow connected to unusual smells and my feeling of rain."

*****

The last person on Tim's "to-visit list" was the late lieutenant Paul Robbins. Tim and Alyssa spent some time at the graveside for Lieutenant Paul Robbins, Tim's flight commander. Tim had called Mr. and Mrs. Robbins and requested to meet together.

Tim and Alyssa stood on the steps of the home of the Robbinses, in Alexandra, Virginia. Tim rang the doorbell. Mr. Robbins opened the door and said, "Welcome to our home. Please come in." Mr. Robins opened the door and extended his hand to Tim.

"My name is Paul. This is my wife, Pat."

"Paul, my name is Tim, and this is my fiancée, Alyssa."

Pat Robbins gave Alyssa and Tim a hug.

The Robbins made Tim and Alyssa feel comfortable as they sat in what was obviously a formal living room. The home would easily be described as a home of a very successful family.

Pat was happy to hear that Tim and Alyssa were engaged. Pat wanted to talk about the wedding plans. In the midst of the excitement about discussing wedding plans, Pat went silent, and a tear appeared on her cheek. Alyssa immediately knew what had happened. Alyssa stood up, extended her hand to Pat, and asked, "Pat, do you mind if we go into the kitchen to talk?"

Paul said, "Tim, our son had a very high opinion of you. He often made reference to you in his letters. From what I have heard, you were honored by our president."

Tim said, "Paul, I had a very high opinion of your son. He was my flight commander, and I am proud to call him my friend."

Paul spoke of his son, Paul Jr., with fond memories and shattered hopes.

Pat and Alyssa returned and invited the men into the kitchen. The ladies had prepared some light snacks and coffee and tea. The kitchen atmosphere was less formal, and the foursome talked about a wide range of topics. In the midst of the conversation, Tim shared how Alyssa's father offered him a job in the Standard Printing Company. Paul seemed to be very interested in the details of the printing business.

As Tim and Alyssa were getting ready to leave the Robbinses, Tim said, "Alyssa and I would consider it an honor if—"

Alyssa cut Tim off. "Tim, Pat and I already worked this out. Paul and Pat are planning to attend our wedding. And I extended an invitation for the Robbinses to sit with our parents at the reception."

Paul said, "Tim, would you kindly take me on a tour of the Standard Printing Company? I would like to see the operation."

Tim said, "Sure. I would love to show you around. Just let me know when so I make sure I'm available. I'm in sales, and I am often out of the office."

Paul said, "What about Monday morning?"

Tim said, "Absolutely. I will be there."

As Tim and Alyssa were driving home, Tim said, "I wonder why Paul is interested in the printing company."

Alyssa said, "I don't know."

On Monday morning, Sandi called Tim on the telephone intercom.

"Tim, you have a Mr. Paul Robbins and two other men here to see you."

"Okay, thanks. I'm on my way."

Tim welcomed Paul with a handshake.

Paul said, "Tim, I hope you don't mind I brought a couple of my associates. Tim, this is Don Sparks and Angel Torres." Everyone shook hands. Paul continued, "Tim, do you mind if we take a tour, and can we talk with your employees?"

Tim said, "Absolutely. I told the owner, Terry Wilson, we would be in the printshop. He would like to meet you after you finish your tour."

Tim took Paul and his associates on a tour of the company. Paul and his associates asked detailed questions of all Standard Printing Company employees. Tim was surprised with the depth of questions and knowledge of the printing equipment by Paul's associates. Mr. Angel Torres spent a good amount of time talking with Sandi.

When the tour was over, Paul asked, "Tim, do you mind if my associates and I have a few minutes together privately? Then we would like to speak with Mr. Wilson."

Tim said, "Sure. You can use my office. I will have Mr. Wilson meet with you in the conference room. It's just across the hall from my office."

Tim asked Terry to meet with Paul Robins and his associates. While Terry and Tim were waiting for Paul Robins and his associates, Terry said, "Tim, do you have any idea what this meeting is all about?"

"No, sir. I have no idea."

Tim introduced Terry to Paul Robbins and his associates.

Paul said, "Mr. Wilson, thank you for allowing us to meet with you and your employees. I'm sure you are wondering what we are doing here today. Let me begin by saying my son was privileged to serve in Vietnam with your future son-in-law. Tim and Alyssa were kind enough to meet with us in what I wish to describe as a family meeting. During our meeting together, Tim spoke highly of your printing company. You have a reputation for running a first-class business. You have been selective in your purchasing of top-quality equipment. When Tim told me you recently installed the latest in a laser printer, I felt it was time to launch a new program. As such, my research group is prepared to discuss a possible business endeavor with you."

Terry said, "I'm okay with having a business discussion, but I want my office manager included in this meeting."

Terry indicated for Tim to go get Sandi.

When Sandi arrived, Paul said, "Mr. Wilson, my associates and I represent a research group established under the direction of the United States Department of Food and Drug Administration. We have been tasked with establishing a standardized global identification system for all products sold on the open markets. We are calling this identification system a Universal Product Code (UPC). The UPC will be a symbol of bar codes encoding a twelve-digit number system for each product.

Terry said, "So you anticipate every product sold in the United States will have its own UPC?"

Paul said, "Yes. And our agency will regulate the specific code assigned to every product."

Tim said, "Paul, you said the UPC will include an encoded twelve-digit numbering system. How will the general public read this coded system of twelve digits?"

Paul said, "The general public will not be able to read the code. We still need to develop a laser reader. We do not anticipate any problems with the development of the needed readers. Our main focus now is to get every product in the entire sales market labeled. The readers will only be useful after all products have a UPC."

Terry asked, "How can we fit into this plan?"

Paul said, "When Tim told me your company purchased the new laser printer, we felt this may be the time to launch the program. Your new printer will be able to produce the quality of a product we need to develop the readers. Our tour of your company gave us the assurance we need to begin the program."

Terry said, "What would be expected of us?"

Paul said, "The three of us will need to go back to our full committee and finalize any proposal, and I am sure you will need some time to consider a detailed proposal as well. However, the three of us agreed to discuss an unofficial action plan."

Terry said, "Okay, give me your unofficial action plan."

Paul said, "We anticipate a very generous contract signing bonus. We anticipate an initial contract for a five-year term. We anticipate you will need to buy a second laser printer and probably a few new employees. We think Sandi will need two additional employees in the office. We will provide probably three of our own employees who will actually assign the encrypted codes for each product. We anticipate building a secure structure on the adjacent property. Which brings me to your assurance that this anticipated plan is not discussed outside of this meeting room. We do not want your neighbors or competitors to jack up their prices just because government money may be involved in the purchasing of land or structures. In addition, our contract will not interfere with your ability to conduct your own printing business. In fact, we anticipate your business will increase substantially when companies submit requests for you to print their packaging with the UPC because they do not have that ability. I know this is a big decision. From what we have seen today, your company is perfectly set up for the launch of our plan. Do you have any questions?"

Terry said, "I like what I hear, but naturally, I need to see the details."

Sandi said, "I need to see what is expected of any additional office staff. In addition, if you have three of your staff working within our four walls, I need to know—no. I mean, they will need to know they will answer to me on their cooperation and healthy contribution to the workplace atmosphere. I will not interfere with their encrypted coding, but they will not be allowed to disrupt our work environment. We have a happy workforce, and I expect it to stay that way. If I say someone needs to be replaced, I want your word you will support my authority and your staff will answer to me."

Paul said, "Sandi, I give you my word your concern will be addressed in the contract. I commend you on the current workplace atmosphere. We could tell by our tour and discussions with your employees that your staff is a happy workforce. Does anyone have any further questions?"

Terry said, "How soon do you think it will take to develop a contract?"

Paul said, "It will not take long. We have been developing this plan for a long time. We know what we need to do. Your company fits perfectly into our plans. I would expect to give you a contract by the end of the week."

Tim said, "Paul, I was on board until you said a governmental agency could develop a contract within a week."

Paul said, "Tim, this is an unusual case. We already have the funding. We have an approved action plan. We are ready to launch, but we just needed the right printer. Your description of this company provided me with the last piece of the puzzle."

Terry said, "Gentlemen, I appreciate your interest in working with us. I look forward to seeing the details of the contract."

Sandi said, "Don't forget my little concern about employees."

Paul said, "Sandi, I will not forget. I will call you when the contract is completed."

CHAPTER 33

Tim was excited to tell Alyssa about the meeting with Paul Robbins and his associates. Tim said, "Remember how we were impressed with Paul and Pat Robbins' home? Well, now I know how Paul could afford such a fancy home. Paul is a big-time government official. Paul and two of his associates came to the printshop for a tour. They spent a good part of the day talking with our employees. After the tour, they met with your dad, Sandi, and me. They plan to make an offer to your father for a big government contract."

Alyssa was pleased to see that Tim was excited about the prospects of a big contract. He had been a little discouraged in his failed efforts to obtain a big printing contract.

Alyssa responded, "So does this mean we will live in a big fancy home like the Robbinses?"

Tim was slow to respond. He then said, "I'm more interested in our life together and less concerned with the size of the house."

Alyssa said, "Me too. I just want to make sure our house has enough rooms for us and our six children."

"Six?"

"Sure. Maybe even seven."

Tim said, "Let's start small, like a house for two. You and me."

Alyssa said, "Let's start with the wedding. We still have a few things to finalize."

"Like what?"

"You still need to purchase your gifts for your groomsmen. We also need to finalize the menu for the rehearsal dinner."

"Yes, dear."

Alyssa said, "That's what I like to hear."

They laughed. Tim tackled her, and they playfully tussled on the floor, and Tim's prosthetic fell off his leg. Alyssa playfully slid the prosthetic under the couch and out of Tim's reach. Tim laughed so hard his eyes teared up, and he tried to belly crawl to retrieve his prosthetic. The two lay on the floor with Tim holding his prosthetic, and he said, "Can we consider three kids instead of seven?"

*****

Pastor Luke Washington led Timothy Sands and Alyssa Wilson in the recitation of their wedding vows. Brett Corson stood with Tim as his best man. Vicki Wilson stood with her sister as the maid of honor. Alyssa's gown was not only magnificent; it was custom made using a portion of her mother's wedding gown and a portion of Margaret Wilson's wedding gown. Tim was handsomely dressed in a charcoal-gray tuxedo while proudly wearing his gold wedding band on his right-hand ring finger. The ceremony ended with a beautiful rendition of the Lord's Prayer.

Mr. and Mrs. Timothy Sands skipped the idea of dancing at the reception. Tim was concerned his prosthetic would only draw unnecessary attention. Alyssa did not want to put Tim in any uncomfortable position. Tim and Alyssa had prearranged with Pastor Washington that he would acknowledge the gold star families in attendance before he offered a prayer. Brett was called upon to offer a toast. Brett offered a warm and moving tribute to Alyssa and Tim.

Brett said, "Family and friends, I am proud to offer this toast to my best friends. To the new Alyssa Sands, we acknowledge your beauty, which goes much further than merely a stunning outward appearance. Alyssa, I'm not a preacher, but I bet I could get an amen from this crowd to acknowledge your sweet soul, your compassion, love, and happy spirit." And the people said, *"Amen."* Brett continued, "To the new Alyssa Sands's husband, we acknowledge your great skill in the pursuit and capture of such a beautiful wife. Your life has been nothing but a failure until today. You dropped out of college to join the army. That was a dumb thing to do. You couldn't even finish a full tour in Vietnam, like me. You couldn't even set two feet on the ground when you returned to this great country. You even failed to report to West Point. Your father-in-law was so worried you couldn't provide for your new wife that he handed you a job for which you had no experience. I tried hard to find something positive to say about you. I tried really hard but could only come up with the way in which you saved my life and the lives of many others. You became my friend when I had no friends. You made it possible for me to be adopted when I had no family. You bought me three books when I had never before owned a book. You demonstrated faith in God with unwavering belief in prayer. I remember the advice you gave to everyone at Cooper's Camp. You said, 'Check your sleeping bags for spiders and your shoes for snakes.' I need to offer you one more piece of advice. Tim, you better check your sleeping bag for spiders and now termites as well." Everyone laughed. Brett continued, "To Timothy and Alyssa Sands, we offer a toast for good health, happiness, wealth, and love which endures, hopes, and never fails. Salute."

As planned, Paul and Pat Robbins were seated with Tim and Alyssa's parents. Paul was curious about Brett's reference to Cooper's Camp during the toast. Paul said, "Robert, can you tell me anything about Brett's reference to a Cooper's Camp? Is that just a boys' summer camp?"

Robert and Margaret took some time explaining the history of their group of friends spending an annual vacation together at Cooper's Camp in the mountains of Pennsylvania. Robert shared how a group of five families joined together to purchase Cooper's Camp. The group of owners continued to call the location Cooper's Camp. Robert also shared that the main house on the property had deteriorated probably beyond repair. The group was planning to change their use of the property by bringing privately owned campers or recreational vehicles for adult sleeping accommodations. They still hoped to maintain the use of the cabins for the kids and grandchildren to sleep together and everyone would still eat together in the mess hall.

Margaret said, "I was totally against trying to get campers or recreational vehicles up the access road. The road isn't even safe for cars. However, I finally gave my approval after the group came up with an alternate plan."

Pat said, "What changed your mind?"

Robert said, "One member of our group is a lawyer. He came up with an agreement with a local farmer. The farmer has grazing land on the opposite side of the mountain. We agreed to repair his fencing and install gates if he would give us a right-of-way to access the camp. We open and close the gates and drive across his land on a dirt driveway."

Paul said, "That sounds like fun. Would your group consider having another couple join in for a week of camping?"

Robert was quick to say, "We would love to have you join us."

Pat said, "Hold on, sweetheart. I'm not sure I like the idea of camping."

Paul said, "I think you will love it."

Margaret let out a laugh.

Judi said, "Margaret, you need to tell us what is so funny."

Margaret said, "Make sure you bring a camper with a port-a-john or a bathroom. The camp only has an outhouse. Ha. Ha."

Judi said, "I will not use an outhouse."

The group at the parents' table began laughing. They made comments and jokes about two-seat outhouses. They were laughing so loud that Tim and Alyssa decided it was time for them to visit their parents' table to see what was so funny.

Tim asked, "Are you kids having fun?"

Margaret said, "Oh, we are having a great time. We have all agreed to join in our family vacation this summer at Cooper's Camp."

Tim said to Alyssa, "I think we just lost control of the reception. Let's cut the cake and get out of here."

*****

Tim and Alyssa enjoyed their honeymoon in the city, which had brought them together. The honeymooners stayed in one of the best hotels in our nation's capital. They asked the hotel concierge about the possibility of a tour of the city. In a matter of minutes, a taxicab appeared. The driver offered to take them on a tour for forty-five dollars. The taxi driver would drop them off at various sites. He would give them ample time to walk through the site and meet them at an agreed spot for transport to the next site. When the driver dropped them off at the Arlington National Cemetery, he said, "Don't stop to look at anything. Proceed to the tomb of the Unknown Soldier to observe the change of the honor guard ceremony. Then take your time on the way back. I will meet you at the front gate in one hour."

Tim said, "Give me an extra hour. I'm getting tired, and I need to stop to show my respects at a few grave sites."

The driver said, "No problem."

*****

Tim began considering what his mother said at the reception. He then said, "Alyssa, I have something I would like to do."

"I'm listening."

"Mom said your parents and the Robbinses are going to vacation with my parents and the entire gang at Cooper's Camp this summer."

"I know. I can't believe my parents agreed to go camping."

Tim said, "I think it's even harder to believe Pat Robbins would agree. I just don't see her as someone willing to give up her luxuries."

"So what do you want to do?"

"I would like to go to Cooper's Camp. I want to purchase a granite marker in honor of my fallen brothers on dust off 786. I want to place the marker next to the flagpole on the crest of the mountain. I would love to have Paul and Pat Robbins see this as a memorial to their son when they arrive at Cooper's Camp."

Alyssa said, "If that's what you want to do, then let's go. I would like to see the camp I have heard so much about."

*****

When Tim was approaching Muncie Valley, Pennsylvania, he came upon a funeral home. He stopped and said, "I'm going to see if the funeral director will give me directions to a monument provider."

Tim found the door open, and he announced his presence. "Hello."

Someone called out from an office with its door open, "Come in, whoever you are."

Tim approached and extended his hand. "Sir, my name is Tim Sands."

The man said, "Tim Sands. Can't say I recognize the name. My name is Todd Woods. How can I help you today, Mr. Sands?"

"I'm trying to locate a monument provider in the area. Would you kindly recommend anyone?"

"That's easy. There is only one provider in the area. I'll write down the address, along with a simple map to follow, since you are not from the area."

"Thank you."

"I can't connect your name with a funeral. Possibly, in exchange for the address to the Solid Rock Monuments, you could help me make any such connection?"

Tim said, "Sorry, no connection to any funeral. I want to purchase a monument in memory of my fallen brothers."

"Noble enterprise." Todd then pointed to a small shadowbox on the credenza. Inside the shadowbox was a small gold star pin with a purple background. Behind the shadowbox was a neatly trifolded American Flag.

Tim said, "I salute you for your sacrifice. I'm sorry for your loss."

Todd Woods didn't say anything. He handed Tim his notes and directions to the Solid Rock Monuments.

Tim said, "Thank you."

Alyssa looked at the map Tim had handed her and said, "It looks like we turn right after we leave the parking lot."

Tim started the car but didn't move. He then had a cold blank look on his face.

Alyssa said, "Honey, what's wrong? You look like you just saw a ghost."

Tim turned off the car.

"Tim, what's wrong?"

Tim said, "I'm not sure, but we need to go back in and ask Mr. Woods a question."

Tim got out of the car and then opened the door for Alyssa.

Alyssa said, "Tim, what's going on?"

"I am not sure."

Tim opened the door and said, "Hello. Mr. Woods, it's Tim and Alyssa Sands."

"Come in, again."

Todd Woods jumped to his feet when he saw the woman with Tim. "Greetings, my name is Todd Woods. Did I mess up the directions?"

Tim said, "Sir, with all due respect, what is the name of your son who died in combat?"

"My son's name was Robert. Why do you ask?"

Tim was shaken and sat down. He asked, "Robert Woods, Twenty-Fifth Infantry Division, Third Battalion, Fourth Infantry Unit, killed in action September 10, 1968?"

Todd seemed to collapse back into his chair. He simply said, "Yes."

Tim said, "Sir, I had the privilege of serving with your son. In fact, I flew as his escort from the battlefield to our base camp."

Todd said, "I was wondering if you lost your leg in combat. I have not had anyone say Robert's name since his mother died."

Alyssa said, "Mr. Woods, I am so sorry for your loss. What was the cause of your wife's death?"

"Broken heart."

Todd took a sip from his coffee cup. He said, "I apologize for my neglect. Can I offer either of you anything to drink?"

Alyssa said, "No, thank you."

Todd said, "I don't remember Robert ever writing about a fellow soldier by the name of Tim Sands."

Tim said, "No, Mr. Woods. I had just arrived in country. I was a medic and had just replaced Robert's unit medic, who was injured in combat."

Todd said, "So you were a medic. That's an honorable calling."

Tim said, "I wish I could tell you more about your son."

Todd said, "I have made peace with my losses. I'm thankful for all that you have done."

Alyssa gave Todd a hug and said, "I wish to give our address and phone number. If you ever need anything, please call us."

Todd said, "Thank you."

It wasn't long before Tim and Alyssa drove into the parking lot of the Solid Rock Monuments.

Tim introduced himself to the proprietor, Jamie Charleston.

Tim looked at the samples of monuments arranged in rows according to size and styles. Tim was looking for something similar to the monument already set at Cooper's Camp.

Jamie Charleston printed out a proposal for the inscription as requested by Tim. It read,

> * In Memorial *
> Army dust off # 786
> Lt. Paul Robbins,
> Flight Commander
> WO2 Mike Porter, Pilot
> Sgt. Rob Gott, Crew Chief
> May 26, 1969

Tim gave his approval.

Jamie asked, "Where is this memorial going to be set?"

Tim said, "I want it set next to the flagpole at what we call Cooper's Camp. I will need to show you its location on a map because I don't have an address."

Jamie said, "Cooper's Camp sounds familiar. Let me look at my files."

Jamie returned with a few documents. He said, "Yep. I have a copy of our billing for a memorial we set there many years ago. I can probably set the monument next week."

Tim said, "Great. What is the cost?"

Jamie said, "Nothing to you. Todd Woods called me and said that he was paying for the monument. He was firm and told me I was not to accept any money from you. So it appears we have our instructions."

Tim was excited to show Cooper's Camp to Alyssa. They walked around the camp and looked in the cabins. Alyssa was not interested in using the outhouse. Tim showed Alyssa the mess hall and the flag-pole with the one monument giving thanks to God for our liberty and freedoms and to those who fought to defend them. Tim and Alyssa sat at a table and enjoyed a picnic lunch. Tim shared a bunch of stories of his experiences he enjoyed at the camp. He hoped their children would have similar experiences.

Alyssa wiped a tear from her eye. She then said, "Tim, I have never seen you so excited about this camp. It obviously has had a positive impact upon your childhood. I am so happy. I can also see why you symbolically brought your fallen brothers to a place you love."

Part 5

The Adventures of a Family

Sometimes you never know the value of a moment until it becomes a memory.

—Dr. Seuss

CHAPTER 34

Summer vacation in August 1970 at Cooper's Camp was unlike any other. The typical five families welcomed Paul and Pat Robbins, Terry and Judi Wilson, and Tim and Alyssa Sands. The Robbinses and Wilsons arrived with brand-new airstream trailers. Tim and Alyssa arrived with a modest pop-up trailer. The vacationers parked their variety of campers in a semicircle on the south side of the mess hall.

Charles Lettice raised the American flag on day one. The entire group shared in recitation of the Pledge of Allegiance. The breakfast was a feast with eggs, pancakes, grits, sausage, bacon, coffee, and fruit. During breakfast, Pat discreetly whispered something to Paul, and he shook his head in the affirmative. Pat then went to their trailer and returned with something in her hand. Paul and Pat Robbins walked together to the monument in memory to dust off 786. Pat placed something on top of the monument. They stood together holding hands for a few minutes and then returned to the mess hall.

The group of vacationers followed the agenda set by Charles Lettice throughout the week. The only deviation in the typical vacation plans was a business meeting. The new owners of Cooper's Camp formed a partnership; and they held a meeting to discuss any matters of concern, goals, or improvements for the good of the camp. Richard Thomson was a lawyer, so he led the meeting. The Robbinses and the Wilsons were welcomed to attend the meeting. The major issue for discussion this year was the unsafe condition of the main house. No one in the partnership had any experience in construction. Therefore, the discussion was superficial with no clear direction on how to proceed.

Paul Robbins asked, "May I have permission to speak?"

Richard Thomson said, "Paul, we welcome any constructive input."

"I do not have any experience in construction, but I do have a lot of connections within the Army Corps of Engineers. The Corps of Engineers issues large contracts to subcontractors. Oftentimes, we can get these subcontractors to do us a favor. With your permission, I would like to make a few calls to see if anyone would send an engineer to assess the building. It may be good to have an expert look at the house."

David Corson said, "I think it's a good idea to have an expert look at the house. It would be a shame to tear the house down if it's not necessary."

Richard Thomson said, "If everyone is in favor of having Paul Robbins seek an engineer to assess the condition of the camp house, say *yea*."

There was a collective "Yea."

Richard was leading to the close of business and said, "Does anyone have anything to say for the good of the camp?"

Paul Robbins said, "My wife and I thank you all for allowing us to join in this vacation. My wife was really not looking forward to the idea of 'camping' even though we brought a bunch of comforts with us in our airstream. We did, in fact, have a great time. Pat told me she wants to return next year if you all would allow us to attend. We also publicly thank Tim and Alyssa Sands for establishing the monument in memory of our son and the crew of dust off 786. This monument has allowed us to feel connected to our son and with you all in this beautiful place. Thank you."

Tim said, "Just for clarification, Alyssa and I arranged for the creation of the dust off 786 monument, but a gold star family paid for it. Mr. Todd Woods paid for the monument in honor of my service with his son, Robert Woods. In addition, we have an announcement to make. Alyssa and I are expecting a baby."

The entire group of vacationers broke out into a cheer.

*****

Five months later, Paul Robbins sent a letter to each of the Cooper's Camp owners advising that he secured the services of a structural engineer and an architect to examine the camp main house. The final analysis of the house determined a structurally weak foundation. The house itself is structurally sound. The engineer's report suggested the raising and leveling of the house and the construction of a new foundation and supporting walls and new pillars on the porch, along with the construction of a safe railing around the porch.

Paul was pleased to report that he secured the services of a construction company in the area to complete the work at a reasonable cost. Paul advised that he and his wife were paying for the costs of these repairs. It is expected that all the repairs would be completed in the spring.

CHAPTER 35

The Standard Printing Company began expanding as Tim landed several big contracts. The government contract for UPC barcodes produced a large number of new customers. Two large contracts involved the printing of manuals for manufacturers of kitchen appliances. Terry Wilson was pleased with the amount of work being produced as well as the superior quality of the outcomes. Terry was also thankful that Sandi had continued to manage a greater number of employees in a manner, which provided for a happy workforce. The additional work necessitated the establishment of a shop foreman, Craig Reed, and another saleswomen, Rebecca Levin. The only problem which surfaced was a devastating health diagnosis.

Terry and Judi Wilson called for a family meeting. Present were Terry, Judi, Vicky and her husband Tyler Hoffman, and Tim and Alyssa Sands and their baby, Tommy.

Terry said, "I wish to begin with a deep expression of my love to each of you. Unfortunately, I have called for this family meeting because I have some bad news. I need to inform you I just received a diagnosis of colon cancer. I have been told it is considered to be at an advanced stage of progression. Therefore, I will be making some short-range plans and hopefully some long-range plans. For the short term, I will be undergoing a surgical procedure and then probably chemotherapy. As a matter of necessity, I am officially giving Tim full authority to run the printing company effective immediately. Your mother and I will still retain ownership of the company. As a matter of long-range planning, your mother and I are going to negotiate a plan for transfer of joint ownership with each of you as family. If there is no interest in a family ownership, we will explore the idea of selling the business. If God allows, your mother and I will fight the

158

good fight, and we will then seek opportunities to travel and enjoy quality time with our grandchildren."

On the following day, Terry Wilson called for an office staff meeting. Present were Terry, Tim, Sandi, Craig, and Rebecca. In addition, Terry had invited his lawyer, Hallie Powell.

Terry said, "I have something to share with you, which will be one of the hardest things I have ever had to do. I need to have surgery for colon cancer. As a matter of due diligence, I am, hereby, giving full authority for Timothy Sands to be assigned as manager in all matters pertaining to the company. Mr. Powell will draw up the necessary paperwork to make Tim's management authority effective immediately. Now, Sandi, please assemble our employees together. I want to talk to everyone at the same time."

Sandi assembled the employees together, as directed.

Terry Wilson said, "Folks, you have been the best workforce any business owner could ever wish to have. I need to tell you our company will be going through some changes. God willing, these changes will result in even greater things than we could ever imagine. First, I need to step aside from management because I am facing major surgery. Timothy Sands will have full authority to manage this company. However, before I hand him that authority, I am directing Sandi to issue a bonus check in the amount of a thousand dollars to each of you."

There was a collective applause.

Marco Winchester called out, "Mr. Wilson, with your approval, can we all gather around in a circle and hold hands and pray over you and the doctors for a successful surgery?"

Terry gave his approval by reaching out to hold hands and moved to help form a circle of prayer. Three employees prayed, and Marco Winchester closed with a powerful appeal for God's healing.

*****

Three years after Tim assumed full ownership of the Standard Publishing Company, Alyssa was experiencing some difficulties with her third pregnancy. Alyssa needed her parents, Mom-mom and Pop-

pop Wilson, to babysit Tommy and Cheryl. Alyssa wanted Tim to accompany her to a doctor's appointment to discuss the latest prognosis. The doctor advised Alyssa that her third baby would be born with Down syndrome.

Tim called his best friend Brett Corson and his wife, Susan, to Virginia for a possible job opportunity. Tim made arrangements for a business dinner date with Alyssa, Brett, and his wife, Susan.

After dinner, Tim said, "Alyssa and I are planning to make some major changes at the Standard Printing Company. I would like to know if you guys are interested in coming on board. First, our company has made a transition to printing manuals for a large number of major manufacturers. Printing is something we do well. Susan, you have expressed an interest in using your education and experience in the development of homeschooling materials. We are prepared to expand our business to include a publishing company. One part of our business will be the publishing side, and the second division will print the materials. I can envision Brett leading the printing side of the business because that workforce is so experienced it practically runs by itself. I can begin the publishing side of the business. Susan and Alyssa can work with me according to the time they may have available."

Alyssa said, "Tim, tell Brett and Susan how we view the business ventures will work with our view of family time."

Tim said, "The printing company has been extremely successful. I do not want the business to dictate our lives. I want the business to support our family in finances and in life. Alyssa and I are determined to take time off for family. I allow my employees to take off for family issues, church events, and community activities. I have a couple of employees who take off from work early for coaching sports teams during certain seasons. Our company even sponsors the teams. If an employee sits down with me and explains their purpose in participating in these activities, I will often approve the activity, with pay. Brett, if you should agree to manage the printing company, I would expect you to support this same policy."

Brett said, "I feel totally inadequate to manage a business in which I have no experience."

Tim said, "Welcome to the front office. Alyssa's dad took a chance on me. I had no experience and couldn't even walk the floor for more than one hour a day. Actually, the trick is to let those who know what they are doing do what they do best. You don't need to tell them what to do. You let them tell you what they are doing and why. You learn from them. In time, you may be able to teach a new employee. Besides, I will still be around. I will step in if a problem comes up."

Brett said, "Can Susan and I spend some time discussing your offer? You have been more than generous in your offer. I just want to have some time for us to talk."

Tim said, "I respect that."

Alyssa said, "We can also have the company help with your moving expenses and set you up in a comfortable home."

Brett said, "Tim, can you give me a ballpark number on a salary?"

Tim said, "Sure. Let's say I will give you a starting salary of double that of your current salary. In addition, we offer our employees a great health plan, retirement plans, and company-wide bonuses."

CHAPTER 36

Tommy and Cheryl Sands went to Cooper's Camp in the summer of 1982 with Mom-mom and Pop-pop Wilson. This was the first time since their marriage that Tim and Alyssa were unable to attend the annual vacation. Alyssa was expected to deliver their third child during the week of vacation. Everyone was comfortable with these arrangements. Tommy and Cheryl were looking forward to a new activity at camp planned by Charles Lettice. Vacationers were advised to bring mountain bikes since Mr. Lettice had identified a bike trail for a new adventure.

Tuesday, August 10, 1982

Today, Alyssa and I were blessed with the birth of our third child at 5:30 a.m. Alyssa is an amazing mother.

Thank you, God, for blessing us with another beautiful child.

The doctors have told us that the effects of Down syndrome would limit our little child. As Alyssa held our daughter, she commented on how precious this child was. We agreed on a name for our newest daughter. She would be named Alana, which means "precious."

Alyssa and I prayed the following:

1. Thank you, Lord, for blessing us with another beautiful child.
2. Lord, help us to be good parents.

3. Lord, bless Alana with the ability to rise above any physical challenges she may experience in life.

Amen and amen.

The Overcomers

Tim made arrangements for the birth announcement to be shared with their children, grandparents, and all of the vacationers. Tim would call Todd Woods. Todd would then drive up to Cooper's Camp and share the birth announcement.

Tim did, in fact, call Todd early in the morning of August 10, with the news of Alana's birth. Todd arrived at Cooper's Camp early enough to participate in the Pledge of Allegiance and to enjoy an outstanding camp breakfast. The birth of Alana was first shared with Tommy and Cheryl and the grandparents and then all the vacationers.

Tommy and Cheryl were so excited about their new sister's arrival; they talked Mom-mom and Pop-pop Wilson into leaving camp for home early. The siblings greeted Alana with kisses and hugs. Mom-mom and Pop-pop Wilson greeted Alana with tears of joy. Tim's parents arrived a day later to welcome their newest grand-daughter. Alana started her life in the midst of a loving family with prayers and support.

The Sands family of five began having a positive impact upon their community, church, and local sports teams. Tim began coaching baseball teams. Tommy began playing sports. Cheryl began playing soccer. Baby Alana began winning hearts with her bubbly personality. Alana grew into the person which reflected the meaning of her name as "precious."

Alana also had the support of her extended family. Brett and Susan Corson moved into a house across the street. Brett accepted Tim's offer to manage the Standard Printing Company while Tim focused on the establishment of a publishing company. Brett and Susan were not only unofficially named as Alana's "Uncle Brett" and "Aunt Susan," but the Corson family also grew through the official adoption of two children. The Corsons adopted a brother and sister duo as new members of their family. Their newly adopted son, Stefan, was the same age as Tommy Sands. Their new daughter, Sophia, was slightly younger than Cheryl Sands. Thus, little Alana had two new "cousins" as part of her support family.

*****

As teenagers, Tommy Sands and Stefan Corson excelled in academics and sports, and they both joined the Civil Air Patrol. As pre-teens, Cheryl Sands and Sophia Corson focused on their appearance, their clothing, and the latest story about boys in their classes. As a young girl approaching first grade, Alana was developing into a loving friend to others, as determined by her. Alana did not like people to touch her or invade her personal space. If someone ran up to her to hug or touch her, she would resist his or her approach. However, if someone were sad or upset about something, Alana would gently approach that person, maybe put her hand on the other person as a manner of comfort. If Alana saw someone who was crying, Alana would approach the person, even a stranger, and place her hand on his or her face to wipe away a tear. Alana had a supersensitivity, a sagacity of empathy. Interestingly, while Alana was typically meek and mild, she would become very aggressive to intervene and attempt to stop anyone from fighting.

Alana had some difficulty with traditional methods of learning. However, Alana blasted through every coloring book given to her, with amazing expertise. If Alana didn't have any coloring book, she would walk over to the printshop to find some paper. She would then draw her own pictures and then color in the images. Alana knew she was not allowed to walk around in the printshop, but she also knew how to test the boundaries by taking two or three steps into the shop just far enough to grab a few sheets of paper. Mr. Frank Beauregard was aware of Alana's desire for paper. When he observed her in the area, he would place a few sheets of paper on a table near the area where Alana could reach. Mr. Beauregard also kept a small supply of lollypops in his locker. When Alana was in the area, Mr. Beauregard would stop his work for a moment. He would retrieve a lollypop and place it next to the small stack of paper. When Alana thought Mr. Beauregard wasn't looking, she would sneak in and grab the paper and the lollypop.

When Alana was around nine years old, she found a new friend. Mrs. Jodie Dorsey was employed as an illustrator in the publishing company. Alana was captivated by Mrs. Dorsey's creativity in drawing illustrations for various publications. Alana was invited to call her new friend, Ms. Jodie. This new relationship grew into a loving sharing of art. Ms. Jodie began challenging Alana by giving her some basic drawing assignments.

Ms. Jodie found that Alana was quick to incorporate new basic drawing techniques into her God-given talents. Alana was not only creative but also had a superb visual memory.

Ms. Jodie said, "Alana, today I want you to think of a dog lying asleep on a porch. Draw the image."

Alana asked, "Can the image include a bird?"

Ms. Jodie replied, "Your assignment is a dog on a porch. Anything else you choose to add is up to you. I didn't limit your image. I just identified the main subject."

Alana went to work with an amazing speed and expertise. It seemed like she knew exactly what the image was going to be before she could even draw it. In less than an hour, Alana had produced an image of a bulldog lying on a pillow. A bluebird was perched on a post of the porch railing. The blue sky had a few puffy clouds with a flock of geese flying in formation. The details of the wooden deck and railing and a rocking chair made the picture almost seem like a three-dimensional painting.

Alana presented her finished drawing and said, "I wanted to draw the dog with one eye open, like he was looking at the bird."

Ms. Jodie said, "That's perfect. Why didn't you draw the dog with an open eye?"

Alana said, "You said the dog was asleep."

Ms. Jodie said, "Correct. When you have a specific assignment, you must follow instructions. You can be creative and still follow the assignment. I didn't say what kind of dog. You chose to draw a bulldog. That's fine. I didn't say the dog was sleeping on a pillow. You chose to have the dog sleeping on a pillow. That's fine. Alana, I think the next time you come over, I'm going to let you try to draw with the computer paint-pad."

Alana smiled and said, "I will ask Mommy if I can come back tomorrow."

CHAPTER 37

Summer vacation in 1990 at Cooper's Camp began to reflect some changes. In the recent years leading up to this vacation, Robert Sands, Charles Lettice, and Robert Thomson had all passed away. Tim and Alyssa Sands, Brett and Susan Corson, and Paul and Pat Robbins had bought into the ownership of the camp. Tommy Sands was unable to vacation with the family, because he was a cadet at the Coast Guard Military Academy in New London, Connecticut. Tommy's military goal was set on flying as a helicopter rescue pilot.

Tim, Brett, and Paul sat together around the firepit while on this vacation one evening and began having a discussion about fellow Vietnam veterans.

Brett said, "I have some fellow veterans who would love to spend a week together up here."

Tim said, "You know, I have some disabled veterans who would enjoy a week up here as well."

Paul said, "We have developed a first-class mountain bike trail. What if we build a couple of handicap accessible dormitories? We could recruit sponsors and volunteers to conduct a week of activities designed to accommodate different levels of abilities. We could purchase a bunch of mountain bikes for the veterans to use."

Tim said, "I could contact Dr. Anthony Campari to see if some medical people would volunteer their services. I could use our staff at work to design an advertisement package to raise some financial donations to cover the costs. Then the veterans could attend at no cost."

Brett said, "I know of a veterans group called the Pathfinders Ministries. I would bet they would be interested in participating in something like this."

Brett said, "Let's bring up the idea at our next camp ownership meeting."

Over the years, Todd Woods established a routine visit with the vacationers on one day, during breakfast. During this vacation, Todd was welcomed with a cheer because he brought a number of fresh doughnuts and sticky buns for all to enjoy. In addition, over the years, Todd learned to share in a private gesture of respect by placing his gold star on the top of the dust off 786 monument, in memory of his son, Robert Woods. Pat and Paul Robbins had established this gesture in a way that each year, Pat would place their family gold star on top of the monument for the duration of their vacation. They did this in memory of their son, Paul.

Brett, Tim, and Paul sat with Todd during his breakfast visit. They shared the idea of hosting a vacation week for veterans at Cooper's Camp. Todd seemed to be thinking of an alternate idea.

Todd said, "Would you guys consider an expansion of your plan?"

Brett said, "Sure. What are you thinking?"

Todd said, "I am not sure if this would work, but I have a close connection with a Christian college in the area. If I could work on a plan, maybe we could host a vacation for veterans, to include disabled veterans, at the college. This may expand the possibilities of activities to include swimming, basketball, and mountain biking. We could maybe use student housing-and-dining facilities. I don't know if this would work, but I have a lot of connections in the community. We could generate a large amount of donations to maybe make a financial donation to the college to offset some expenses."

Paul said, "I like this idea. I'm sure I could contact a number of government officials and defense contractors for donations."

Tim said, "I have a number of manufacturers who would love to make donations in exchange for public recognition."

Todd said, "Let me see if I can arrange for a meeting with Dr. John Hancock. He is the president of Muncie Valley Grace Christian College."

Tim said, "Let me talk with Hallie Powell. As my lawyer, he is probably going to advise us to form a nonprofit incorporation. This would provide for the appropriate processing and accountability for donations."

*****

Salute to Veterans Inc. was established and began making plans to host its inaugural Mountain Blast Adventure for Veterans at the Muncie Valley Grace Christian College on July 1 to July 6, 1991. The initial event would be limited to a hundred veterans to enable the planners to properly manage the events.

Dr. John Hancock was pleased to allow the college facilities to be used for such a unique event. He was able to establish a reasonable cost for the use of the college facilities for veterans and volunteers. As college staff learned of the event some offered to volunteer their services as lifeguards, cooks, and athletes. The college choir offered to perform during the proposed opening and closing ceremony.

Todd Woods was able to secure several business donations and local volunteers for the first Mountain Blast Adventure for Veterans. Todd also secured the local high school band to play the national anthem for the opening ceremonies.

Paul Robbins secured a few large donations from defense contractors. Paul also called in a couple of favors. As such, he was able to ensure the participation of the West Point Honor Guard for the presentation of the American flag during the opening ceremonies.

Tim Sands obtained a few corporate sponsors. The sponsors were excited to be involved in this adventure. The sponsors pledged to increase their support if the event would grow into an annual occurrence. Tim's printing and publishing company became the primary sponsor.

Brett Corson made contact with the Pathfinder's Ministry in North Carolina. He was able to easily identify and invite one hundred honored guests.

One key activity which ensured a success in securing a large amount of donations and volunteers was the advertising plan. Early in the planning for the Mountain Blast of Adventure for Veterans, Tim had a meeting with his illustrator, Jodie Dorsey. Tim wanted

Jodie to create a logo, posters, banners, and mailers for advertising and securing donations.

Tim said, "Jodie, I want you to focus on this project and use all our contacts to get this information out to the largest number of people possible."

Jodie said, "No problem. I will work up a few ideas for your review and approval. What is my time frame for this project?"

Tim said, "Consider it was due yesterday."

Jodie said, "Okay. I have an idea on how this can be done quickly and with your approval."

Later in the day, Alana walked into Ms. Jodie's workstation.

Ms. Jodie said, "Alana, I have a huge project you need to work on as a big surprise for your father."

Alana said, "I like to surprise my daddy. What can I do?"

Ms. Jodie said, "I need you to draw a picture of a man riding a mountain bike. However, the man will have both a prosthetic leg and a prosthetic arm."

Alana said, "Can the man look like my daddy when he wears his shorts?"

"Yes. Exactly. And the man will have a short-sleeved shirt so we can see that he has a prosthetic arm."

Alana said, "That will be easy because I have seen our friends ride mountain bikes at Cooper's Camp."

Ms. Jodie said, "I also need a second picture, which may be a little harder. I need you to draw a few men in wheelchairs playing basketball. Some of the men will not have any legs. Some may only have one leg. And one needs to be throwing a basketball. Some men will have red shirts, and others will have olive-green shirts."

Alana said, "Okay, that will be fun."

Alana didn't need any further directions. Jodie began developing a distribution plan with mailers and return envelopes for the Salute for Veterans Inc. She also began to design a logo. She was thinking of a soldier in silhouette saluting an American flag.

Within one week, Jodie called Tim and asked if he would review and approve the promotional materials for the Salute for Veterans project.

Tim said, "Do you want me to come over to your office?"

Jodie said, "No. We will come to you."

"'We'?"

Jodie said, "Yes. Alana and me."

Tim wasn't sure why Alana was coming over, but maybe she was just visiting with her friend, Ms. Jodie.

Jodie knocked on Tim's office door.

"Come in."

Jodie and Alana walked into Tim's office. Tim was sitting at a small conference table. Alana ran over and sat in her father's empty office chair.

Tim said, "Young lady, you better come over here and give me a hug. Then you can play boss."

Alana jumped out of her father's chair and ran to give him a hug.

Tim said, "Jodie, I hope my little precious isn't being a problem for you today."

Jodie said, "Tim, your little precious is not a problem for me, yet."

"What do you mean 'yet'?"

Jodie said, "Let's go over your review of the materials first. Then I want to talk about Alana."

"Okay."

Jodie began by showing Tim the proposed logo. The logo was a soldier in silhouette saluting the American flag. Tim was happy with the logo.

Jodie then said, "Alana, show your father your first poster."

Alana removed a large poster from the cardboard tube and handed it to her father. The poster focused on a man riding a mountain bike. The man had a prosthetic leg and arm. However, the details were so clear the drawing almost looked like a photograph.

Tim looked at the poster and said, "Alana, did you draw this poster?"

"Sure."

Tim was overcome with joy and amazement. The poster was fabulous. Tim looked at Jodie with a questioning look.

"How did she..."

Jodie said, "Tim, look at the second poster."

Alana rolled out the poster, which highlighted a man with no legs, sitting in a wheelchair, while throwing a basketball to a fellow team member. The team members with the ball were wearing olive-green Army shirts. The opposite team was wearing red Marine shirts. Tim just admired the poster, and tears began appearing on his cheek.

Alana's sensitivity kicked in. She reached out to wipe away her father's tears. She said, "Daddy, I'm sorry I made you cry."

"Sweetheart, these are happy tears. I am so happy and proud of you."

Jodie then had to wipe away her tears, as well.

Tim said, "Jodie, how much did you do on these posters?"

"I took about five minutes describing two ideas to Alana. She drew the two sketches in about two hours. She then went to work on the paint box. Tim, Alana did all the work on these posters. You asked about Alana being a problem for me. Yes. I'm beginning to worry about her taking my job away from me."

Tim said, "No. I think I need to reconsider your pay scale. I knew you were helping Alana. However, I didn't realize how much you have taught her."

Jodie said, "I love working with Alana, but her raw talent is beyond my ability to teach her anything. I think you may need to consider some kind of advanced art classes or private lessons with an artist."

Tim said, "Maybe my little precious just needs to be herself and enjoy her talents given to her by God."

While Tim and Jodie were talking, Alana made her way back to her father's office chair. Jodie noticed Alana's move and said, "Tim, with all due respect, you better be careful because it looks like your daughter is after your job, not mine."

Tim laughed. He said, "Jodie, look for the most advanced equipment available to upgrade your office in art technology. When you identify the best technology, submit a purchase request for two. I want you and Alana to have the best equipment available. In addition, you can expect to see a significant increase in your salary, effectively immediately.

Jodie asked, "What about the posters?"

"The posters are perfect. I just want a cover letter to explain the details of the planned event. I want you to distribute these posters to every one of our customers, to every veterans' organization you can find, to every news outlet, and to our governor's office, every state and federal official. I will contact everyone in the Salute to Veterans Inc. for a contact list from each member. I will call Alyssa and Susan and have them pull together a group of volunteers to help you with the distribution. I want these posters to be distributed to every business in our community."

CHAPTER 38

The first annual Mountain Blast Adventure for Veterans was a huge success. Not only did this event provide an opportunity for veterans to enjoy some challenging activities, but it also began a movement to honor and welcome home Vietnam veterans. The Vietnam War had generated fierce opposition and protests to the war and, by extension, a disdain for the soldiers who fought in that war. The Mountain Blast Adventure seemed to provide an atmosphere of acceptance and appreciation for the sacrifices made in service to our country.

Dr. John Hancock, president of Muncie Valley Grace Christian College, was asked to give a challenge during the closing ceremonies.

The following is a small part of Dr. Hancock's comments: "During this adventure for veterans, I was curious about something. In the planning stages for this event, I noticed a small detail in one of the advertising posters. In one of the posters, I saw an image of a man with a prosthetic leg and prosthetic arm riding a mountain bike. As a civilian, I could look at that poster and wonder if the person lost his limbs in combat or in a car accident. I would have no way to know for sure. However, in the poster, I noticed the image of the bike rider wearing a Purple Heart. That little detail spoke volumes to me. Most veterans do not advertise their medals. In fact, most Vietnam veterans do not even advertise their prior military status.

"My investigative curiosity drove me to further explore this little detail. I was able to discover that Alana Sands created this poster. With her permission, I am able to disclose my conversation with this amazing young lady.

"I said, 'Alana, have you ever seen a military person wear a Purple Heart medal?'

"'Sure. A soldier has a ribbon on their uniform for every medal they receive.'

"I instantly realized I was in the presence of someone smarter than me. I would need to reframe the question. 'Alana, when you drew the image of a man riding a bike, why did you include the Purple Heart medal?'

"'The image of the man in the poster was not wearing a uniform. If I didn't include the medal, no one would know he was a soldier. My daddy has a prosthetic leg. When my friends say things about my daddy, I always tell them he was a soldier. Every year, we vacation at Cooper's Camp. We have families who place a gold star on top of a monument in memory of their soldiers. I place my daddy's Purple Heart on top of the monument that honors soldiers who defend the freedoms and liberties God has given us. My daddy lost his leg while serving as a soldier, and I love him.'

"The Bible tells us about the words and wisdom of children. I share this little story at my own demise. Not only do you know this young lady is smarter than me, but now you know you should ask her to give the closing comments at your event next year.

"In closing, I thank you for serving in defense of this great nation. I thank you for defending the freedoms and liberties given to us by God. It has been an honor to have our college host this event. I hope we can do this again next year."

At the close of business on the last day of the Mountain Blast Adventure for veterans, Tim Sands and Brett Corson met with Dr. John Hancock to settle the final payment for use of the college facilities.

John Hancock said, "Gentlemen, this event generated such a positive response we received so many donations and volunteers that we can probably reduce your remaining balance due."

Tim said, "Dr. Hancock, we also received a tremendous amount of donations. Given the fact that we already wrote the check for the full amount as per our prior agreement, let's just settle for the remaining balance due for the full amount."

John Hancock said, "Well, this is good news. Maybe we can use some of that money to purchase some additional sports equipment and special handicap bicycles."

Brett said, "We were also thinking of purchasing some supplementary equipment for the next event. In addition, our organization is interested in establishing a student scholarship fund. With your approval, the Salute to Veterans Inc. is seeking to fully fund two students in the Muncie Valley Grace Christian College. We were thinking of a scholarship for any student seeking a military chaplaincy career and a second student scholarship for a student seeking a military medical career."

John Hancock said, "Wow. That type of a scholarship will be attractive for incoming students. Tim, since we are talking about students, I would like to ask you a couple of questions about your daughter."

Tim said, "My daughter Cheryl is planning to seek a career in nursing like her mother. However, if she should choose your college, we would never allow her to apply for the scholarship. That would be a serious conflict of interest."

John Hancock said, "We would love to have your daughter Cheryl as a student. However, I was thinking of your daughter Alana."

Tim said, "Oh, sorry, I wasn't thinking of Alana."

John Hancock said, "I would like to explore the idea of asking your daughter Alana if she would consider being a guest instructor for one of our art classes. Apparently, Alana is advanced in using the latest in art technology. I would love to invite Alana to introduce our students to some of her techniques. I am thinking of inviting your daughter for a one-week appearance as a guest instructor."

Tim said, "Wow, that is something I would have never thought of as a possibility. Alana is certainly talented, but she is not comfortable in the presence of strangers. I don't know if your proposal would work."

John Hancock said, "Tim, sometimes, a gifted person is reasonably comfortable in his or her environment while not particularly comfortable in other social settings. Would you consider talking about it with your wife and daughter?"

Tim said, "Would you consider having two for the price of one?"

"I am listening. What do you have in mind?"

Tim said, "I need to talk to my illustrator. Maybe, Jodie Dorsey and Alana could come as a tag team."

When Tim arrived home, he went directly to see Jodie Dorsey.

Tim said, "Jodie, did you locate the latest in art technology?"

Jodie said, "Yes. As per your instruction, I have the purchase order prepared for two units." She handed Tim a folder with the details for the purchase of two desktop computers, software applications, and advanced printers.

Tim said, "Thank you. I will review the purchase order and get back to you."

Tim was determined to purchase four units. Two units would be donated to the Muncie Valley Grace Christian College art department, regardless of any guest appearance by Alana Sands. Tim changed the purchase order to reflect the purchase of four units.

CHAPTER 39

Tim was ready to make some major business decisions. Tim had a few business discussions with Alyssa, and they agreed to bring Brett and Susan Corson into these business considerations. Tim and Alyssa invited Brett and Susan for a business dinner discussion.

The friends enjoyed a great dinner at an exclusive establishment.

Tim said, "In order for me to write off this dinner as a business expense, we need to shift the discussion to our businesses. I see a major shift in our industry. With the advancements of personal computers, printers, and the Internet, our printing industry is facing a massive reduction in services. In the past, we printed thousands of packets of information for appliances. Now the manufacturers are making the same information available to their customers via the Internet. We are still publishing schoolbooks, but our customers are seeking more e-books. Therefore, we need to make some adjustments in our business plans."

Brett said, "What are you proposing?"

Tim said, "Alyssa and I are ready to make some changes. We want to transform the large commercial printing company into a retail business model designed to print small- to moderate-size projects with a fast turnaround time. We could print letters, invitations, envelopes, business cards, banners, funeral prayer cards, and local election materials. The smaller retail business model could occupy a downtown storefront. We could hire a small staff and purchase easy-to-use large-volume color printers. This business model could then be replicated and expanded through business franchises. We could keep the one Standard Printing Company to act in support of the publishing company and to our small fast-print franchises. Then if any one of the franchises lands a large printing job, it could be sent to our main printers."

Brett said, "How do I fit into your plans?"

Tim said, "Brett, as you know, I have treated you as an employee."

Brett said, "And I appreciate how you have paid me beyond my wildest expectations."

Tim said, "It's time for Alyssa and me to bring you and Susan in as owners. I need you to oversee both the printing and publishing companies. You will need to manage an appropriate level of downsizing without killing the businesses. I will develop the opening of maybe three fast-print stores. All four of us will be consulted on the development of these new retail stores. Once we have a working system in place, we will move forward in developing a franchise prototype."

Brett asked, "Do you really think there is a market for a fast-print downtown retail store?"

Tim said, "I do."

Alyssa said, "Did I ever tell you how I love to hear those two words?"

The four all laughed.

Tim said, "You loved the words 'yes, dear.' I was the one who liked the words 'I do' when you said them on our wedding day."

The dinner conversation slowly drifted away from business and began to focus on kids, college, and careers. Tim and Brett would later agree on the appropriate level of business ownership. The Standard Printing Company and the Standard Publishing Company would now include a third branch, the Standard Fast-Print Company.

CHAPTER 40

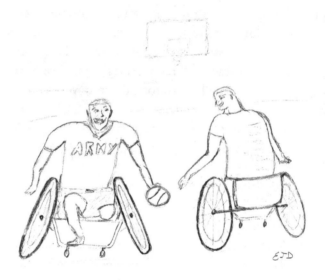

The fifth annual Veteran's Blast at the Muncie Valley Christian College was a great success. The college used every available space to accommodate three hundred veterans and one hundred volunteers. In addition to several sports challenges, the veterans were offered various opportunities for personal growth.

Participating veterans were invited to attend seminars on leadership, community service, art therapy, overcoming post-traumatic stress disorder (PTSD), and business opportunities.

Tim and Brett conducted a seminar on business opportunities for veterans to manage their own Standard Fast-Print Company. Tim and Brett were able to secure donations for veterans to have some start-up money to manage their own fast-print business.

Jodie Dorsey and Alana Sands conducted a seminar on art therapy. Alana had grown into a young lady who was comfortable with veterans. Veterans with missing limbs did not distract Alana. A prosthetic leg or a missing leg was no big deal for her to deal with because she had helped her daddy with his prosthetic all of her life. Alana had learned how to share her love for art without judgment on someone's ability or lack of ability to draw or paint or design on the latest form of art technology. Alana earned the respect of the veterans, and it was well-known that no one dared to say or do anything disrespectful toward Alana. The offender would be subject to extremely harsh retribution by many other veterans.

Paul Robbins arranged for several defense contractors to set up display booths and offer job opportunities.

The biggest sports challenge was a basketball tournament. Each of the military academies sent their respective basketball team for a playoff competition. Through a blind draw, teams were assigned as competitors. West Point played against the Air Force Academy. The West Point team was victorious. The Coast Guard Academy played against the Naval Academy. The Naval Academy was victorious. The Naval Academy played against the Merchant Marine Academy. The Naval Academy was victorious. The outcome of these games set up a playoff between the Army and Navy academies. The Army team was victorious and earned the right to play against the veterans. Therefore, the final game was the Army cadets against a pickup veteran team. Both teams were required to play while using wheelchairs. The teams were given the rules that players could not use his or her legs/feet to steer the chair. In addition, each player must dribble the ball after two pushes on the chair, and the player with the ball must continue with this sequence. The game between the Army and veterans was a highlight of the week of events. The veterans won the wheelchair basketball game.

Part 6

The Adventures of an Overcomer

Show me someone who has done something worthwhile,
and I'll show you someone who has overcome adversity.

—Lou Holtz

CHAPTER 41

Debbie West knocked on Tim's office door.

Tim said, "Come in."

Debbie said, "Tim, I'm sorry to bother you, but I need to leave work to go check on my mother, Lara. I'm worried that something is wrong."

Tim said, "Sure. No problem. What makes you think something is wrong?"

"She's not answering her phone."

Tim said, "Do you mind if I go with you? I don't like the idea of you going alone."

Tim rose from his seat without waiting for a response.

When Debbie unlocked and opened her mother's door, Tim was shocked with the overwhelming smell of gas fumes.

Tim yelled at Debbie, "Get back. Get away from the house. Go out to the street, and call the fire company, *now.*"

Debbie hesitated.

Tim pulled Debbie by the arm and yelled, "*Go to the street, and call 911.*"

Debbie started to run to the street. Tim ran into the house. Tim found Debbie's mother lying on the kitchen floor. Tim picked up Debbie's mother and began to carry her out of the house when the explosion occurred.

Debbie and her mother were grateful that Tim risked his life to save Lara Williams. However, Lara was facing many surgeries to address her severe burns.

Tim was facing burn surgeries as well. However, his blindness would be permanent.

CHAPTER 42

While Tim was in recovery from the fiery blast, his daughter Cheryl moved into a position of leadership within the family businesses. Brett welcomed Cheryl's involvement. She seemed to demonstrate a natural talent to learn quickly and gain respect from the workforce.

Tim and Alyssa had some long talks about the future. Tim made it clear he would not be defined by his disabilities. In fact, he even had an idea for the start of a new business. Alyssa listened and was ultimately supportive. During one particular discussion, Tim brought up his recurring and haunting dream.

Tim said, "Sweetheart, I think I finally made a connection to my recurring dream."

Alyssa said, "So the bright light was the gas explosion. The darkness was your blindness. The gas was the smell. What about the rain in your dreams?"

Tim said, "First, go back to the smells. In my dreams, I smelled something unusual. Try mixing the smell of gas and flesh burning. Now I can identify what I smelled in my dreams. Then in my dream, I could feel the rain. In the explosion, the water pipes were broken, and I was drenched with water, which, by the way, helped suppress the burning."

Alyssa said, "So how does your connection with the dream and the explosion help you, or us, for that matter?"

Tim said, "This is a very important connection. See, I think the event was important to save Lara Williams's life. We know we are God's workmanship, created in Christ Jesus unto good works, which God ordained that we should walk in them. I was just doing what God set before me. I have always referred to myself as an overcomer. You know, I saved a lot of lives as a medic. I lost a leg and part of my hand. We overcame the losses, and my life has been great. I was put in a position to save Lara's life. I lost my eyesight. We will overcome.

Alyssa responded with a kiss. She said, "Did I ever tell you how much I love you?"

Tim said, "Let me think about…"

Alyssa punched him on his arm.

Tim said, "Hey, you can't hit a blind cripple."

Alyssa said, "You better be careful. I can now make your life more miserable by just hiding your prosthetic."

They hugged, and Tim said, "We are going to be okay."

Alyssa said, "I know."

CHAPTER 43

Tim arrived at work to the cheers of the entire workforce of the combined businesses. Tim had asked for a gathering of all the workers because he wanted to make a major announcement.

Tim said, "First and foremost, thank you all for your prayers and cards and well-wishes during my recovery. I am sure you are all thinking this is going to be my farewell speech. Well, in fact, it is not. I am not going anywhere."

The workers all broke out into cheer and applause.

"In fact, I want to announce the creation of a new adventure within our publishing division. I have spoken with Brett and Cheryl, and we have agreed to launch an audiobook publishing division. As many of you know, I love to read books. I now realize that I will be limited to listening to books. Therefore, we will develop a first-class audio publishing division."

There was a loud cheer and another round of applause.

"Mr. Sands, may I say something?"

Tim said, "Yes, you may speak, but I don't recognize your voice. Please tell me who you are."

"Sir, it's Lara Williams. My daughter, Debbie, invited me to this meeting. I believe everyone was expecting you to announce your retirement. I am so glad you are not. I wish to thank you publicly for saving my life. I am so sorry you experienced blindness as a result of saving my life and the life of my daughter. 'Thank you' seems like such insufficient words, but I do thank you from the bottom of my heart."

Tim said, "Thank you, Lara. Now, I was about to tell you all to get back to work, but I seem to smell some food. It is possible that my comanagers decided to plan some kind of a party without my approval?"

Brett spoke up. "Tim, Cheryl and I have declared this to be a celebration day. No work today. We have our entire workforce and their families here for a celebration. We also have some guests that will introduce themselves to you and your family as you all sit at the head table."

Tim said, "Let the party begin."

CHAPTER 44

Tim and Alyssa accepted an invitation to address a group of students at a local high school. Tim was excited to bring boxes of books to give to the students.

Mrs. Penny Westcott introduced Mr. Timothy Sands as a decorated war veteran, business owner, and father to Alana Sands. The students all applauded because they all knew Alana.

Tim said, "With me today is my beautiful wife, Alyssa. From your response to my being introduced as Alana's father, maybe you should have invited her today."

Mrs. Westcott replied, "We tried to get Alana, but we had to settle for you."

The students all broke out into laughter and then a loud applause as Alana appeared on the stage. She walked over and gave her father and mother each a kiss on the cheek.

Tim said, "I was asked to share with you on the topic of a lifetime of adventures. I really want to keep my remarks brief and see if you have any questions for me or my wife or daughter. Just for your information, we have another daughter, Cheryl. She is a manager in one of our businesses. We also have a son who serves as a lieutenant in the Coast Guard. He is a pilot flying a rescue helicopter.

"My story begins with my first journal. My parents gave me a journal while on a vacation, where I was introduced to my lifelong best friend. At the end of this vacation, my friend and I wrote the same entry in our respective journals. I have asked my wife to read the entry."

Alyssa read,

Last day of vacation—August 10, 1957

The following is a list of things Tim and Brett enjoyed while on vacation at Cooper's Camp:

1. Country: We live in a great country. We raised the flag. We thank God for freedom and liberty, and we honor those who defend our freedoms.
2. Family: We have great families and friends. It is fun having vacations with family friends at Cooper's Camp.
3. Faith: We found out that God answers our prayers. We found out that God knows what will happen because he is in charge.
4. Books: We found out that reading is fun. We can travel into the past or future with book stories.
5. Friends: We have friends because we are friends.
6. Leaders: We see leaders (Dad, Mom, Pastor Cooper, Charles Lettice, Richard Thomson, Ms. Linda) and want to be leaders like them.

Vacation this year has been great.

Goodbye.
Overcomer

Tim said, "I have been blessed to have adventures in each area of life described in that journal entry. I love this country. I consider my military service as a privilege and an honor. I have friends because I am a friend. I have faith in God, and I have seen his answer to prayer. I love books. Our businesses have published and printed a great number of books. Now because of my blindness, I have created a company to produce audiobooks. My wife and I brought boxes of books for you all today. I have been among some of the greatest leaders in our country. I have served with leaders in government, business, and education. Which brings me to the topic of leadership in your lives.

"If you were to look at the journal entry my wife read, you would see where a teacher wrote a big red letter F on that page. That teacher was not very understanding and certainly not very encouraging. However, I used that failing grade as a stimulus for proving her wrong. I trust that you will not let setbacks, failures, or disabilities define you. Now do you have any questions for my family or me? Please tell me your name before you ask your question."

"Mr. Sands, my name is Liam. What did you do in the military?"

Tim replied, "Liam, I served as a medic. My primary mission was to treat our wounded servicemen on a medevac helicopter. We were basically a flying ambulance."

"Mr. Sands, it's Liam again. Did you receive any combat medals?"

"Yes, Liam. I did receive an Army Commendation, a Bronze Star, a Purple Heart, and I'm most proud of my medic combat badge. I was also promoted from an enlisted man as a sergeant to that of an officer as a lieutenant."

"Mr. Sands, my name is Anthony. Did you lose your eyesight in combat?"

"No, Anthony. I lost my leg and part of my hand in combat. However, I lost my eyesight while rescuing a woman from a gas explosion in her home."

"Mr. Sands, my name is Lois. When your wife read your journal entry, she ended it with a reference to an 'overcomer.' What does that mean?"

"Lois, that's a great question. I like that you were observant enough to pick up on that reference. In the Bible, we find a number of references to people being called overcomers. There are also rewards to those who are overcomers. I have always tried to avoid letting bad circumstances or disabilities define me. Yes, I lost a leg, but that's not who I am. Yes, I am blind, but that's not who I am. I am an overcomer. I lost my ring finger on my left hand but not my right hand."

"Alana, my name is Brenda. I love your art. What is the meaning of your name?"

Alana said, "Brenda, I was born with Down syndrome. God gave me special talents in art. My parents named me Alana because it means 'precious.' Actually, I think my parents are the ones who are precious."

While the questions were proceeding, Mrs. Penny Westcott took Tim's journal.

At the end of the question-and-answer period, Tim thanked everyone for his or her attention and meaningful questions.

Mrs. Penny Westcott said, "Mr. Sands, we appreciate your service to our country, your contributions to our community and schools. We can't give you much for your time with us today. However, I hope you will accept this little token as a gift from all of us."

Mrs. Penny Westcott handed Tim back his journal opened to the same page Alyssa had read earlier.

The red letter F was covered with a yellow smiley face sticker. Next to the smiley face was a blue-ink A+.

Alana said, "Daddy, the F is gone. You got an A+ in your journal entry."

CHAPTER 45

Tim was looking forward to his scheduled meeting with Mayor Lewis Clark. However, Tim did not know the purpose of this meeting. Tim's inner office telephone rang.

Tim answered the inner office telephone, "Yes."

The company receptionist said, "Mr. Sands, Mayor Lewis Clark is here for your 10:00 a.m. meeting."

Tim said, "Great. I will be right there."

Tim knew his way around the office complex. He was able to traverse by sounds, by memory of the number of steps between offices, and by slightly touching the walls and feeling door trims.

Tim walked into the reception area and greeted Mayor Lewis Clark.

Tim said, "Mayor Clark, welcome to the Standard Companies."

Tim heard the mayor get up from a chair. This movement enabled Tim to turn toward the mayor and offer his hand.

Mayor Clark said, "Thank you."

Tim said, "Please come down to my office."

Tim turned and led the way to his office.

Tim offered Mayor Clark a seat at a small worktable. Tim's office was very appealing and featured many citations and awards on the walls.

Tim asked, "Mayor Clark, would you like some coffee, tea, or water?"

Mayor Clark said, "No, thank you. I'm fine."

Tim said, "Okay, great. Before we get into the reason for this meeting, I want to thank you for the work you did on securing the improvements to Garden Road. For years, that road would be flooded before the weatherman would even forecast any significant rain.

Mayor Clark said, "Yes, I know. That road would flood because of ice or snow melts from the mountains. Rain was just another contributing factor to the problems on the road."

Tim said, "Okay. Please tell me why you wanted to have this meeting?"

Mayor Clark said, "I need your help. No, let me say this with a different focus. Our community needs your help. In this next election cycle, we are losing two of our most dedicated councilmen. Our friends from the opposite side of the aisle are seeking to promote two candidates who will not work for the betterment of our community. We believe you would bring intelligence, community pride, common sense, and a business mind-set to the position of a councilman."

Tim said, "Well, I was not expecting this. I thought you were possibly looking for a donation for some worthy project, which I would have gladly supported. I have never had any interest in politics."

Mayor Clark said, "The word *politics* has a negative connotation because some elected officials seek to make themselves the focus. You mentioned earlier about the repairs made to Garden Road. Politics didn't get the job done. Hard work and commonsense got it done."

Tim said, "Are you sure you don't need a contribution for some worthy project? Maybe even a contribution for an unworthy project? I will gladly make a contribution."

Mayor Clark said, "No. This is an appeal for you to step up to the plate and hit a homerun for the home team."

Tim said, "Mayor, do you realize how silly that sports illustration is when applied to a blind man?"

Mayor Clark laughed and said, "Yeah, that was probably not the best illustration I could have used."

Tim said, "Mayor, I will come back to you with another baseball illustration. I was expecting a slow pitch, but you threw me a curve ball. It is an honor to even be considered for such a respected position. However, I will need some time to think about it. I also need to discuss the idea with Alyssa."

Mayor Clark replied, "Understood. However, we have a deadline to submit the required petitions with a specific number of valid voter signatures in support of your candidacy. Please consider giving me your answer as soon as possible."

Tim said, "I will give you my response as soon as possible."

*****

Tim, Alyssa, and Alana were enjoying a steak dinner. Tim began the discussion of a possible political career by saying, "I had a very interesting meeting today with Mayor Lewis Clark."

Alyssa said, "Was he looking for a donation?"

Tim said, "No. Actually, he is looking for a pound of flesh."

Alana asked, "Daddy, what does that mean?"

Alyssa added, "Yes, dear, what does that mean?"

Tim said, "The mayor is looking for a new councilman because they will be having two retirements coming up this year."

Alyssa asked, "And the mayor wants you to run as a councilman in the next election?"

"Yes, that's what he wants."

Alana asked, "Are you going to be the mayor?"

"No, Alana. They need a councilman. Mr. Lewis Clark will remain as the mayor."

Alana said, "I can vote this year. I will vote for you."

Alyssa said, "Well, Tim, you have at least three votes."

Tim asked, "Does that mean you all are in favor of this decision?"

Alyssa said, "Yes. You will make a wonderful councilman."

"I have never used my disabilities as an excuse to not do something. However, the possibility of dealing with letters, documents, and policy statements may present a challenge."

Alana said, "Daddy, I can help you like I do at work."

Tim said, "Alana, you are a big help to me at work. However, reading documents to me or for me in public may be a challenge."

Alana asked, "Are you trying to tell me this challenge is something we can't overcome?"

Tim smiled and asked, "Is this where the student becomes the teacher?"

Alana said, "This is where we become a team that can't be beaten."

CHAPTER 46

The newspaper headlines wanted to focus on Timothy Sands as the first blind man to be elected as a councilman in Harrisonburg, Virginia. In every newsperson interview, Timothy Sands made it clear his election had nothing to do with his disabilities. Rather, he wanted to focus on his past accomplishments and his future goals and expectations. Tim put an end to the constant questions about his blindness by writing an open letter in the newspapers to the news media. Tim wrote, "If and when a newsperson should begin an interview with questions pertaining to my blindness, the interview will end at that unanswered question. If, however, the newsperson should ask relevant questions pertaining to my official duties, proposals, or accomplishments, then at the end of the interview, I will gladly entertain personal questions."

The swearing in ceremony for Councilwoman Cindy Abbott and Councilman Timothy Sands was scheduled for noon on January 1, 1997. In preparation for the swearing in ceremony and the first scheduled council meeting, Tim and Alana requested a meeting with the town administrator, Jonathan West, and solicitor, Mickey Thomson.

Tim said, "Gentlemen, I requested this meeting to clarify my intentions and explain the inclusion of my daughter in my official duties."

Mickey Thomson said, "Please proceed."

Tim said, "As you know, my blindness occurred later in my life. As such, I have never had any training in reading braille. In my business world, I use my daughter Alana as my reader. In some cases, I have Alana read a letter or report to me. In some situations, Alana will read my letter or statement or policy to my staff or the public. I wish to continue this practice in fulfilling my duties as a councilman."

Mickey Thomson said, "I see no reason you cannot use your daughter as a reader. However, I would object to having her vote on your behalf or represent you in any proxy manner. If Alana were to read something publicly on your behalf, you should follow her reading with a statement that the reading on your behalf is true and accurate as intended."

Tim said, "That's fine. I would also ask if Alana and I could arrive about a half-hour prior to any scheduled meeting to review the agenda and documents related to the meeting."

Jonathan West said, "No problem. In fact, after you are sworn in, I will give you a set of keys for access to the municipal building. You will have access to your internal mailbox any time you wish."

*****

Mayor Lewis Clark conducted the reorganizational meeting for the Harrisonburg town council. During this meeting, Mayor Lewis Clark gave a report on the many accomplishments of the previous year and a long list of potential projects, goals, and aspirations for the future. The mayor spoke highly of each of the councilmen and thanked the two retiring councilmen for their years of service. Mayor Clark welcomed Councilwoman Cindy Abbott and Councilman Timothy Sands.

After taking the oath of office, the two new councilpersons were given an opportunity to share their thoughts. Cindy Abbott expressed her gratitude for the support she received from the voters and pledged to serve the community to the best of her ability. Timothy Sands gave praise to God and gratitude for the support he received from the voters, his family, and fellow veterans. He also pledged to serve the community to the best of his abilities.

*****

During the next eleven years, Timothy Sands established himself as an elected representative of the people with a positive reputation of having respect, success, and compassion. One procedural accomplishment that proceeded without disruption was the smooth reading of letters, documents, policy statements, and budgets by Alana for her father. One unknown practice was Alana's allowance, paid to her by her father, which happened to be the same amount of money as his councilman's salary.

CHAPTER 47

Summer vacation at Cooper's Camp in 2008 was very similar to the same experiences as in previous years. Over the years, the buildings were somewhat improved. The mess hall was transformed into a modern cafeteria-style dining hall with air-conditioning. A large pole barn was transformed into a basketball court. Tennis courts were the latest addition. The family ownership of the camp had changed over the years. However, for now, the camp still maintained a ban on any electronic equipment. The outhouses were replaced with actual bathrooms and running water. Not "hot" water. Sometimes, the hot-water heaters failed to keep up with the demand. Quiet time and reading were still encouraged.

Tuesday's camp activities drew to a close with a beautiful sunset. Several of the adults were sitting on the deck of the main house overlooking Muncie Valley. The sun disappeared beyond the furthest mountain, and the black sky lit up with starlight. A slight chill caused some of the women to wrap themselves in sweaters or light blankets. It looked like a storm was brewing and rolling in over the mountains. The conversations were light, fun, and uplifting.

As the evening progressed, clouds began to cover the starlight, and this change ushered in darkness, and families began to turn in for the night. Tim and Alyssa were the last two sitting on the deck.

Alyssa said, "Tim, I'm getting a chill. I think I'm ready to turn in."

Tim said, "If you don't mind, I want to sit here for a little longer."

Alyssa said, "Okay."

She gave him a kiss and let Tim sit alone on the deck.

Around one o'clock in the morning, a clap of thunder awakened Alyssa. When she turned over in bed, she realized that Tim was still not in bed. She thought, *Could Tim still be sitting on the deck with a storm coming in over the mountain?* Alyssa got out of bed and looked out the window. Tim was still sitting in his deck chair. Alyssa went to the door and quietly called out, "Tim, it's time to come to bed."

No response.

Just like at home, she often had to wake Tim up from his chair to get him to go to bed.

She wrapped herself in a bathrobe and walked barefoot to Tim and shook him.

No response.

She knew immediately that Tim was dead. Alyssa's nursing experience kicked in, and she knew by his rigid body that he had been dead for a couple of hours. There was no reason to administer CPR. There was no need to call 911. Tim's health was failing over the past year. He was taking his medication, but Alyssa surmised that Tim had suffered a heart attack.

Alyssa sat down next to Tim. After a few minutes, reality began to set in, and Alyssa whispered a prayer, "Thank you, Lord for the amazing husband, and father to my children, you gave to me. Thank you for allowing him to depart this world in a place he loved and with those who loved him."

For some reason, Lisa woke up. She wasn't sure if she heard something or not. For whatever reason, she decided to look out the window. Lisa saw two people sitting on the deck chairs. She was not sure, but it looked like Tim and Alyssa. That's where they were seated earlier. Lisa opened the door and softly asked, "Alyssa, is everything okay?"

Alyssa simply said, "No."

Lisa heard the "no" and ran back to her room to wake up David.

"David, wake up. Now! Something is wrong."

David heard the word "wrong." He started to wake up and said, "What?"

Lisa put on her robe and slippers. She said, "Get up. Now. Something is wrong with Tim and Alyssa."

Lisa ran out to the deck and quickly realized what was wrong. She saw Alyssa crying and Tim slumped to the side of his chair.

When David arrived, he also realized the situation and placed his hand on Tim's shoulder, as if to somehow comfort him.

David knelt down by Alyssa and held her hand.

Lisa walked back into the house to wake up all the adults sleeping in the main house. She and David then woke the adults sleeping in trailers or recreation vehicles.

In a matter of minutes, a large group of friends were all assembled on the deck. It was quiet. No one was talking, but you could hear the faint sounds of crying and sniffling. Amazingly, there was a transformation in the sky. The storm clouds dissipated and rolled away like the movement of a curtain revealing a deep dark sky with thousands and thousands of stars, some twinkling and some shooting in various directions. The moon began peeking over the mountain ridge. The darkness of the night was majestically overcome by light.

Someone in the group quietly began to hum an old hymn. Soon others joined in humming the hymn. Finally, the group of friends transitioned into a choir and began singing the old hymn "It Is Well with My Soul" loudly and in harmony.

The singing of the hymn was followed with silence. No one said anything.

Finally, Alyssa broke the silence. She said, "Lisa, earlier you asked me if everything is okay and I said no. I would like to change my response to that question. My answer is now a yes. My heart is heavy, but everything is okay."

Alyssa got up and thanked everyone for his or her love and support. She then said, "Lisa, will you come with me to tell Alana and Jodie?" Tommy and Cheryl were not attending this camping trip. Alyssa would need to call them. However, Alana and her coworker Jodie Dorsey were sleeping in a recreation vehicle in the camp RV circle.

Lisa nodded in agreement and stood up.

David said, "I will get my spotlight and tag along as an escort."

*****

The funeral for Timothy Sands was a challenge for the Hoffman Funeral Home. The number of anticipated guests would be the greatest amount ever assembled by this funeral home. Veteran organizations from across the nation planned to send delegates. Business owners from major companies were planning to arrive by private and corporate jets. The federal government was sending delegates. State and local elected officials were planning to make an appearance. Special arrangements were made for the West Point honor guard to stand guard to play bilateral echoing taps and to present the folded American flag to the spouse of the deceased. Pastor Paul Charlesworth was trying to create a reasonable list of individuals whom Alyssa could approve to speak during the eulogy. The Pathfinder Ministries Inc. and the Salute to Veterans Inc. were identified as preferred recipients of donations in lieu of flowers.

Four hundred guests were invited to a luncheon at the Center State Country Club. The Standard Companies provided for the luncheon following the funeral services. This event also provided an opportunity for additional speakers.

One particularly memorable speaker was General Edward W. Muller. General Muller stated that he was a graduate of West Point, class of 1973. This was the class in which Sergeant Timothy Sands was assigned. In fact, in 1969, Plebe Edward Muller was assigned to billet with Plebe Timothy Sands. When Timothy Sands failed to report for his induction into West Point, the story of his survival and subsequent battlefield promotion to the rank of second lieutenant was a legendary message of perseverance for other cadets to emulate. General Muller stated, "I was honored to meet Timothy Sands at a veterans event sponsored by the Salute to Veterans organization and hosted by the Muncie Valley Grace Christian College in Pennsylvania. When I told Timothy that we had been assigned to the same billet, had he reported to West Point as intended. Timothy told me that his God-assigned detour resulted in his meeting a beautiful young lady by the name of Alyssa. I was shocked to hear that Timothy Sands was more excited about meeting a pretty nurse with a bed pan rather than sleeping and showering with a handsome man like me."

Everyone laughed.

CHAPTER 48

Two weeks following the funeral of Timothy Sands, Mayor Lewis Clark requested a meeting with Alana Sands. The two met in Tim's office at the Standard Companies.

Mayor Clark said, "Alana, our community is grieving with you and your family. In this grieving, we also wish to honor your father for the number of years of service to this community."

Alana asked, "How can the community honor my father?"

Mayor Clark said, "I think the greatest honor we can do is appoint you as a councilwoman to fill the remainder of your father's elected term. Alana, you know the details of every project we are working on. You know the budget inside and out. You know how your father would have voted on policy and projects currently under consideration."

Alana said, "Isn't this where you make some kind of sports illustration about my hitting a home run?"

Mayor Clark laughed and said, "You are your father's daughter."

Alana said, "I need to talk to my mother."

*****

The newspaper headlines wanted to focus on Alana Sands as the first woman with Down syndrome to be appointed as a councilwoman in Harrisonburg, Virginia. In every news interview, Alana Sands made it clear her appointment, as a councilwoman, had nothing to do with her disabilities. Alana made it clear to the media if and when a newsperson should begin an interview with questions pertaining to her syndrome, the interview would end at that unanswered question. If, however, the newsperson should ask relevant questions pertaining to her official duties, proposals, or accomplishments, then at the end of the interview, she would gladly entertain personal questions.

One daring reporter commented to Alana that her position on interviews was very similar to that of her father, as he related it to his blindness.

Alana said to that reporter, "Yes, my position is very similar to that of my father's. However, let me add one more condition. If you ever make a disrespectful comment about my father, I will never grant you another interview."

When Alana Sands was officially appointed as a councilwoman, she was given the oath of office. She was then afforded an opportunity to make a comment.

Alana said, "I thank Mayor Lewis Clark and the entire council for their vote of confidence in my fulfilling my father's term of office. My father lived a life full of adventures. He taught me many important things about life. However, the greatest lesson in life he passed on to me is to never be defined by your disabilities. God has blessed me with talents, and, yes, I have needed to face challenges. However, I am an overcomer, and I pledge to serve this community to the best of my ability."

You can't go back and change the beginning,
but you can start where you are and change the ending.

—C. S. Lewis

E. James DuBois

The Pathfinder, a novel, Christian Faith Publishing, copyright 2017

The Sanctuary Cabin, a novel, Christian Faith Publishing, copyright 2020

Called to Work, an autobiography, Christian Faith Publishing, copyright 2021

ABOUT THE AUTHOR

E. James DuBois is a graduate of Philadelphia Biblical University (now Cairn University) and the California Graduate School of Theology. He has served as a pastor, teacher, school administrator, state prison chaplain, and coordinator of chaplaincy services, and retired from the New Jersey Department of Corrections as an assistant divisional director. Jim DuBois is a decorated Vietnam War veteran. He served as the director for the New Jersey Department of Corrections Critical Incident Stress Management Team and led this team in direct support to the New York—New Jersey Port Authority in New York City at ground zero following the attack on our country on September 11, 2001. Jim and his wife, Christina, have been married for fifty-three years. Their two sons are married. They have been blessed with seven grandchildren. They now reside in Kissimmee, Florida.